THE DESERT AND

Jorge Barón Biza

The Desert and its Seed

Translated from the Spanish
by Camilo Ramirez

Afterword by Nora Avaro

A NEW DIRECTIONS BOOK

Manufactured in the United States of America
New Directions Books are printed on acid-free paper
First published in 2018 as New Directions Paperbook 1406

Library of Congress Cataloging-in-Publication Data
Names: Barón Biza, Jorge, 1942– author. | Ramirez, Camilo A., 1985– translator.
Title: The desert and its seed / Jorge Barón Biza ; translated by Camilo Ramirez.
Other titles: Desierto y su semilla. English
Description: New York : New Directions, 2018.
Identifiers: LCCN 2017041792 (print) | LCCN 2017049304 (ebook) |
ISBN 9780811225816 | ISBN 9780811225809 (alk. paper)
Classification: LCC PQ7798.12.A678 (ebook) | LCC PQ7798.12.A678 D4713 2018
(print) | DDC 863/.64—dc23
LC record available at https://lccn.loc.gov/2017041792

10 9 8 7 6 5 4 3 2 1

New Directions Books are published for James Laughlin
by New Directions Publishing Corporation
80 Eighth Avenue, New York 10011

To Dr. Sylvia Bermann and
my aunt with an aunt's name,
María Luisa Pando de Sabattini.

YOU ARE HERE FOR YOU caress this idea
of flesh like freedom under the sway of darkness
do not burn it with the air of nostalgia
fleeting wishes, the challenge of insubordination
lightening, no waiting, they give you what you dare ask
so you don't die from old wounds.

You are here among your brothers who answer
though you can barely hear them in pages that reveal
the abundance of silence
their beauty protects every movement of your eyelids
its penury is the enigma that is admirably one's own
decipher it with those lips separated by their dark line
the beam of the sensible disposes of it on the members
purging your luck drive to despair your locus reemerged
in the space without consolation you are the most important guest.

—Federico Gorbea (1985)

I

MOMENTS AFTER THE ATTACK, Eligia's complexion was still symmetrical and possessed its rose glow, but minute by minute her facial lines began to curl: lines that had been smooth until that day, despite her forty-seven years and the plastic surgery that had shortened her nose. That small and voluntary cut—which for three decades had conferred on her an air of audacity—was becoming a symbol of resistance to the great metamorphosis of the acid. Her lips, her eyelids, the lines of her cheekbones were transforming to a malicious cadence; curves were materializing where none had been before, while the unmistakable features of her identity were vanishing forever.

Eligia's naively sensual face began to part with its contours and colors. Beneath the original features, a new substance was emerging: not a sexless face, as Aron would have wanted, but a new reality beyond the necessary resemblance of a face. Another genesis had begun to happen—a system of unknown laws.

Those who saw her every day in August, September, October, and November of 1964 witnessed how this face's matter had been completely liberated from its owner's will and could now take on any new form, adopt the hues of the most intense twilight, dancing in all directions, while, at its center, the coquettish nose stood resistant to the changes around it.

It was an agitated time, a time of flux in which the colors of the flesh, free of any form, evoked the blurred spots that filmmakers use to represent the unconscious, in the worst and most candid sense of the word. These were colors that transcended culture, mocking any medical technique that tried to subsume them under an organizing principle.

As we drove away from Aron's apartment to the hospital in one of the lawyers' cars—the lawyer who, before the meeting, promised me nothing bad was going to happen—Eligia tried to take off her clothes, which were soaked in acid. The neon lights of the city flashed across her body. A streetlight brought us to a stop on Lavalle Avenue, and a crowd of pedestrians began to cross despite the honking. Some got curious and tried to glance inside the car, unsure if they were witnessing something erotic or fatal. The flickering lights washed over the metal of the car and Eligia's body. The corner cinema was showing *Irma la Douce*, and an enormous poster of Shirley MacLaine flanked the box office. Red and violet letters ran across it in cursive. Shirley in a miniskirt—the kind only whores wore at the time—held a volatile purse.

Eligia wouldn't scream; she just kept tearing off her clothes, moaning in a low voice. I would have wanted her to scream with all her might so people around the car would stop their stupid smiles and let us through, but Eligia only moaned with her mouth closed as the treacherous moisture in her clothes burned the palms of her hands. Aron had thrown the acid at her eyes—his intention had been to blind her and ensure he was the last thing she would ever see—but the back of her hands had protected her sight with a quick motion that betrayed the apprehension she had been feeling all along. Her palms, spared at first, now burned in this smoldering striptease as we rushed her to the ER.

Back then, I did not know her well, though I had always felt a curious tenderness toward her, so committed to her work, so serious. She had worn short hair for most of her life as a badge of modern womanhood, and also to showcase her full lips and strong jaw. A fine layer of *rouge* always accentuated the sensuality of her mouth. Her lids rested on her eyes with a weary weight, but her gaze had always been alert and full of life. She was proud of her tall forehead, which she tried to make seem even wider by wearing her hair back.

Her face was evidence of her history, the Presotto bloodline—poor Italian immigrants—and her obstinate faith in reason and the power of knowledge. Now the "constants" of her face were vanishing.

We were both laconic. During my childhood, a Polish governess always intervened in our daily lives. Eligia acted indifferent, always focused on her research and politics. But as an adolescent, I understood that her distance couldn't be explained entirely by the presence of the governess. When we went into exile in Montevideo and I started attending a German boarding school, Eligia was out of the picture and remained just as distant. She would visit me every other weekend, and listen to my stories with a faint smile, or staring at me with her head slightly cocked to the side, but she rarely answered my questions. If she did reply, it was with an unrelated query of her own ("Why don't you like the humanities? Are they teaching you Latin?") or with an "I don't know." I took these answers as incomplete figures, as if unfinished business remained between us.

When I was fourteen, we returned from Montevideo. Four years later, when Eligia and Aron separated again, I decided to stay with Aron in the capital. Eligia accepted a teaching position in her native province in the mountains, and we rarely saw each other after that.

She sat on the front seat of the car, moaning without screaming, and it wasn't my fault: I had warned her that Aron had changed during those last few years I had lived with him, that they had been away from each other longer than any time before, and he had become dangerous.

I leaned over her left shoulder, and soaked a few drops of sweat or acid with my handkerchief. The fabric yellowed as if the cotton had turned to silk. Night shadows enveloped this side of her face with a dark violet veil, and only the pearl white of her eye pierced through that darkness, the desperate gaze fixed on a point beyond the windshield, searching for an end to this torturous journey. When I leaned back on my seat, all I could see in the rearview mirror was the whiteness of this eye and the blotch of intense purple on the lower lid surrounded by shadows. This side of Eligia's face was a mystery boiling in the dark.

A few moments later, I nervously leaned forward again, this

time over her right shoulder, where the other side of her face was illuminated by the cinema's light. The eye, awash in neon lights, had the same fixated look of its counterpart in the shadows. I whispered, "We're almost there," though neither of us had asked the lawyer where we were going. I noticed a thick yellow on her cheekbone, and a second spot with the same hue between her eyebrows, touching the boundary where the light no longer reached and likely propagating beneath the shadows on the other side. Varying tonalities of purple composed what remained of the visible half.

I got out of the car to disperse the crowd, but I wasn't able to. It was then that I had my first complete vision of Eligia's transformation. Looking through the windshield, the two halves of her face came together: silent violet, on one side, and metallic yellows and purples on the other. I also saw the desperate stare, the bloated eyelids, and, for the first time, her mouth, which, in the shadows, as well as under the light, was tinged with the same magenta tone, as if the boundary between light and dark didn't exist in this particular zone. This crimson color encroached on the violets and purples with the same intensity, and her lips seemed to possess a radiance of their own. Their width and color recalled a clown's mouth, although they remained still.

At the clinic, she was given a tranquilizer and taken to the emergency room. I was ushered to the aseptic cafeteria and offered a whiskey. Minutes later, when I asked for a third drink, they looked at me with annoyance. Clearly, they didn't appreciate the good customer they had landed; so I took my business to the bar at the corner. You can always find a bar close to a hospital, a hole that smells somewhere between disinfectant and soot; a frontier where we are forced to confront the horrors of life that took us there, including those we have so doggedly cultivated for ourselves. But at the time I didn't know any of this.

For four months I went back to that bar daily, in fact, I was there several times a day, yet I was never able to strike a conversation with someone. A hundred and twenty days, and I didn't manage to make a single move on one of the nurses or maids frequenting the place after work or during their breaks. It was hard to tell if women did not want to talk to me for whatever reason, or if I was just out of my element in this place where people try to resume life after pulling a sheet over a dead body.

I returned to Eligia's room within two hours. There she lay, dozing off with a look of bewilderment. Now and then, she took a deep, involuntary gasp. I asked if she needed anything.

—Nothing. Take care of yourself—she whispered.

She made no mention of Aron. The burns were turning a darker shade of purple in the large center zones, where a grave matter was thickening. Beyond the purple, yellow hues occupied the boundaries between the wounds, accentuating the richness of the central tones. Eligia's body shuddered and heaved, the pain was autonomous, just as pleasure had surely been in better times. But where pleasure had acted with grace and clarity, pain was heedless and did not know or care to spare those parts of Eligia's body that had escaped the attack: causing confusion, it rushed through every limb and vessel, boasting about the harm it produced.

The next morning, once we had settled in the recovery room, a relative arrived to tell me the police had broken into

Aron's apartment and found him with a bullet wound in the head. —Probably for the best! His character wasn't suited for prison—he said.

—Actually, he was in prison several times.

I was the only one who had lived with Aron during those last few years and I always knew his was not going to be a happy ending. I hated his outbursts of violence, every day more extreme, and his novels, which I considered quite kitsch—I didn't even bother to read the one completed shortly before his death—but I also couldn't help but admire his fighting courage, his willingness to risk everything, even his life, at any moment. Everyone talked with reverence about his legendary temerity, even those who had been at the receiving end of his anger. When they told me he had committed suicide, I felt a curious reverence and thought of a fallen warrior who dies by his own code, though I was still horrified by his aggression. I was also assailed by the inevitable question that comes when people we know well take their lives: how and to what extent were we accomplices? I forced myself to abandon that concern immediately. I intuited the threat of example, the simple idea of restoring the order of things with another bullet.

But not I. When I went to live with Aron, I had gotten to know him in a way that I hadn't been able to when his presence in my life depended entirely on the ups and downs of his relationship with Eligia. Those last few years he got worse by the day. My contempt for him only grew stronger, although deep inside I was always in awe of him. I decided to re-create myself as the exact opposite, to embody everything he was not: no violence, no resentment, no anger. Because I was no saint, I practiced apathy from early on.

* * *

After the relative left, the head doctor came into the room. He sat down and observed Eligia in silence, and she stared back with a hopeful look. At first, he remained in contemplation, snug in his starched lab coat which had his initials embroidered on it. Finally, his eyes filled with imperious questions, as if trying to make sense of the painful sight to no avail.

—How is your stomach? —he asked, studying the chart on the clipboard the nurse was holding for him.

Eligia's voice was low but firm.

—Good.

—It's very important. We have to take good care of it. That's where you have all the nutritive substances that will repair the damage. —Yogurts, fruit juices, vitamin supplements—he said to the nurse.

—Eligia always had an iron constitution. —I added.

—I want you to wash her skin four times a day with the special solution—he said after looking at me intently. —It's mineral water with sulfur, copper, arsenic, and other elements. We must stop this disintegration.

He pointed with some concern at the damp gauze covering the abscesses. —We must nourish the body so Nature can restore it. Those mineral baths will bring her, once again, in contact with the elements. Also, at night, leave the window open and let the light from the stars and moon wash over her body as well. How are you related to the patient?

—Doctor, I don't think she will get much starlight from here. If I open the windows, all we'll get in the room is soot, and we'll also hear the other patients moaning.

—Eh?... Some people never understand.

—He's right. You can't really see the stars from here—said Eligia, but the moon ... Last night I woke up ... and there was a bit of moonlight.

—Eligia—I said to her after the doctor left—a reasonable person like you! Don't let me down. You start with the moon magic and end like Aron.

—A reasonable person? —she asked, her voice growing weaker. —That makes no sense ...

Her voice, nasal and drowsy, seemed to be sinking into itself.

—It only made sense before ...

—Before what?

But Eligia did not answer.

Her treatment began the next day.

—Acid is a very special thing—the doctor said after the first surgery when he saw me in the waiting room, though he seemed to be addressing some invisible audience.

—We don't get a lot of burns like this—he said slowly. —At this early stage we can't do the skin graft. We must continue removing the necrotic tissue until the acid can be placated. Don't think I want to do this. It's a process of exposing the impudence inside. Burns that are caused by fire can be covered right away; the sooner you do it, the better: nature returns to a logical course by herself. As you know, we let things heal naturally, without too much intervention. But please know in her case, I won't sleep until I can start the skin implants and cover that whole delirium.

—How long will this process take?

—I don't know. But we must be certain that the acid has lost its power, or the skin graft won't take, there won't be hemostasis.

—But, more or less …

—I would wait twenty days, perhaps fifteen, it depends … After this, grafting the skin will take a few months. What a job I've chosen! He leaned against a wall and drew a blank stare.

—Uncertainty is the curse of this profession—he said.

Back in the recovery room, Eligia was missing a section of her cheeks, and both her hands were bandaged. They had fastened her wrists to the bed. The doctor didn't want her touching her face, not even while she slept.

Thus started Eligia's utter dependence on those around her. The nurses assisted her with efficiency. Someone removed the mirror from the bathroom, and, by tying her hands, they took away her ability to create an image of her face by way of touch. From that moment on, she only knew what was happening to her body through her imagination, fed by loose words from those who assisted her.

Tiny streams of blood would trickle from the depths of Eligia's cheeks irregularly, running over the vivid flesh without skin and only becoming visible upon reaching the white bed sheets. I remained by her side, ready to press the sheets lightly with a handkerchief and soak the moisture before it stained the immaculate whiteness. This task became an obsession. When I failed, the liquid expanded ever so slightly in the cotton before turning a brownish gray. I would try to clean the spot, but always managed to make it worse. Then, I wouldn't rest until a fresh set of sheets was brought to the room. The presence of even the smallest stain represented for me the gravest fault.

During the first few weeks, there was nothing of permanence on her face. While some sections caved in, others swelled up like overripe fruits, promising the juice drained from the cavernous hollows surrounding them. I tried to remain hopeful, but every day it became more difficult; what had once resembled an apple sprouting from her cheek morphed into a red pear before becoming an immense strawberry. Her body was changing in a rhythm of chasms and compressions. This capacity of the flesh for transformation perplexed me. I tried to project logic on what I saw, but calm only came when I accepted everything that occurred as incomprehensible and regenerative, a force that rekindled the very essence of matter every time Eligia came back from the operating room.

I had the vague sensation of having seen something like that juxtaposition of fruits in a piece of art. But now I was the unwilling witness to a capricious and mercurial substance that didn't bother erasing or polishing its own sketches.

Fifteen days went by. The front part of Eligia's neck was shortening little by little. I kept rearranging the pillows so the scorched tendons weren't overstretched. Face and body were close to each other, but without a connection, as if some whim had brought them together.

Something incredible was happening to her cheeks. The partial ablation left contours of flesh that increased the depth of the cavities, where the bubbling of colors offered a false exuberant sensation, like the violent painting of an artist intoxicated with a strange power.

Every morning after surgery, at the bottom of the wells excavated by the surgeons, the vibrant colors of the first day reappeared—those of fresh wounds, signifiers of life and a promise of healing. At the beginning, I tried to convince myself there was a harmonic beauty to this conflagration: tones that defined each other's value simply by their juxtaposition.

Certain zones of different colors had the same saturation, and, when there were differences of intensity, they compensated for each other, so an intense purple, for instance, was usually surrounded by a soft violet. If two sections were thrown out of balance so one color ended up dominating another, in the next surgery the situation was reversed.

Whenever colors withdrew into one of the new caverns opened by the surgeons, I paid close attention to the abyss of each cheek, observing their evolution and hoping that harmony would reemerge from the fresh brushstrokes. Thus, I was introduced to the secrets of negative space, the apse without carvings or statues. There, the wounds had a secret life of their own, hidden by the thick contours. These borders, and the cavity they surrounded, formed a space that was becoming deeper each time, and, at the base, each suture seemed to be on the verge of bursting with a vital force that sprang forth from the wounded flesh, revived time and again by the scalpel. The daily scraping generated a form of life that was foreign to body and treatment; there was an autonomous origin of the organic substance that had been liberated from the order of things. The laboriousness of chaos is contagious.

Copious flowering eventually gave way to rock. After two weeks of removing necrotic tissue, they began the first skin transplants. The rhythm of the surgical interventions relaxed, and the visits to the operating room became less frequent in the next three months. The blaze was eclipsed by darkening scabs. The era of color was ending. The time of form had arrived. Across Eligia's skin, lines began to draw unexpected paths. The currents of acid returned after a cunning delay, making their way through the flesh, eroding it, transmuting life into geology—not a sedimentary or horizontal geology, but a trace of volcanic activity cooled down with pretensions of eternity, stable, fixed, and inexpressive like the desert.

The exterior had assumed an importance that competed with the interior. The new form taking shape on Eligia no longer modeled itself exclusively on bone; a new structural principle acting from the surface now wrestled for control. Muscular tissue was adapting to a system of laws, where the contraction and expansion of skin were as important, or even more so, than the joints or skeletal support, as if the bones had lost part of their structural role when they were scraped of flesh and now had to compete with the implants for the ultimate form of the body.

The day of the attack, the acid had reached Eligia's face from below: she had stood up, along with her lawyers, convinced that her meeting with Aron was over, though she still showed some apprehension. She was hopeful that the matter was finally resolved—at last, after so many years, the divorce was a reality. With a smile on his face, Aron remained sitting as he reached for a pitcher that seemed to contain water. The streaks of acid were thus oriented in a way that contradicted the law of gravity.

The transformation of flesh into rock concealed the bright colors. I understood that the mirage of metaphor was over. Aron's attack had converted Eligia's whole body in a single negation. It wasn't easy to construct figurative meanings upon it. The fertility of chaos had abandoned her. As the months went by, I began to understand the full implications of this, but it was only much later that I realized how the impossibility of seeing metaphors on her flesh became, for me, the impossibility of thinking in metaphors about my own feelings.

The daily fruits ceased to ripen. A general hardness invaded Eligia's face; the protuberances stabilized into an inexpressive lunar landscape. But with this rigidity, the caverns and hollows took on a new sense: the petrified flesh endowed her features with a stillness that allowed for relations to be drawn between one form and another. With these fixed relations, the pedantry of certainty and perspective returned, allowing me to analyze the situation from a purely spatial and impersonal vantage point, and thus avoid being assailed by sentimental considerations. I performed my observation abstractly, focusing not on the hand that threw the acid or the suffering of the victim, not on the hate or love that motivated the aggression, but in the spatial relations of Eligia's face. If necessary, my eye would dissect the burnt skin down to fragments so minute, they lost the human implication of what had happened. I concentrated my attention on these minute spaces, articulating relations that could bring coherence to what had happened there.

Before, the ephemeral fruits that sprouted all over Eligia's body had invited touch to verify their unexpected form, under the excuse of soaking up the blood or plasma pouring from them. The subsidence and fracturing that eventually appeared demanded scrutiny and examination: not only because that's what was required by the incredible structure revealing itself, but because what was perceived in this petrified stage was much more abstract—thus more irrefutable and intangible—than the fascinating fruits of the previous period.

The facial landscape expelled colors and adopted the configuration of those holes found in the ashes of Pompeii, sites where a human being suffocated, consumed by the eruption, voids where only the spectator's imagination could see the flesh existing in them; these holes the sacrilegious archeologist thought of filling with plaster. Just like the surgeon, the archeologist captured a horror that wouldn't let you look away, returning to the clear manifestation of a brutal cruelty, a reminder of what destroys us and still poses a threat.

The precision of the rock, even in ruins, presented itself like the eternal reverse of all human form, the limit—terrifyingly immediate—of our illusions, the nothingness, that encroached with the meticulousness of a geometrician parsing the mud we forget we are. That is how the passage from the hallucination of appearance to the unmistakable regime of this new substance operated on her.

Every now and then, when the anesthetics and tranquilizers began to wear off, and Eligia experienced an instant of full consciousness, she reconstituted her body, and tore from those fragments (now controlled by a hermetic law that kept her hostage) a glimmer of oneness, an "I won't give up," summoning a tenacious dignity in the face of the process eroding her.

I told myself that the new rigidity of space in Eligia's face frustrated Aron's plans: by burning her, he hadn't managed to eliminate the flesh he loved, in fact, the act of demolition had sublimated it, as occurs when structures become historic ruins. Just as any eye reconstructs the incomplete geometry of tilework, I, too, reconstructed the minuscule fragments of her face. My vision re-created from memory the current ellipses of her face, and that remembrance intensified what was no longer visible.

Despite the wrist restraints, Eligia began experimenting with movement. These were small, localized movements that she practiced, I thought, to begin forming a kinesthetic idea of her new body in the absence of other senses. Back then it didn't occur to me how anxious she must have been to see what had happened to her. I thought it made no sense to let her confirm the full gravity of the injury; I feared it would be too much, and the doctors and nurses agreed. It seemed better to keep her in a state where she could still feel determined to recover at any cost, even if she didn't fully grasp what had occurred. Years later, I thought of the unspeakable torture our cowardice must have created with the best intentions.

When Eligia moved, within the minimal range allowed by the wrist restraints, her features clearly indicated that something impossible had occurred to her: no matter how intense her suffering, her reality was no longer convincing. The condition of her new body deprived her of all joy and pride, and bound her to her fate with an absolute intention: to overcome her situation. Unable to see or touch her face, she could only think about her body as a territory under construction: something that didn't yet exist, but was being prepared for existence. She compartmentalized a present reduced to pure suffering, and refused to assign any reflective or existential connotation to pain. To come out of this one, she knew she had to aim in one direction and stay the course no matter what.

She did not ask about the technology they were using on her; she was more interested in tracking her progress. Any sign of improvement brought her enormous relief. Her mind was absorbed in the future. No action, no object, nothing mattered to her during that time unless it could provide a lifeline to the other side. That need for the future played a positive role, not only because it was essential and constant, but also because it erased forever her obsession with perfection and grounded hope on rationality.

That is how the serpentine efficacy of the good works on us, the passage from the ephemeral to God.

My sister did not come to the capital. She was still too young, and we decided it was better for her to stay in the provincial city where she had been living with Eligia for the past four years. My brother had to assume responsibility for the family finances so we could afford the expensive medical treatment. Without much discussion and by default, I was left in charge of Eligia's care.

I have always hated to feel responsible for others. Now I was responsible for Eligia. At the clinic, I made up artificial tasks, never bathed, and never slept on the guest bed. Occasionally, I went to Aron's apartment to shower and change clothes. Fearing him, I had moved out after a heated argument one month before the attack.

I had wandered the city homeless for twenty days after that argument. At night, very late, when the cold of winter emptied the streets of people, the city squares reemerged as gardens. A taste of barbarism remained in the air, as if the space had been plundered—broken streetlights, trash blowing in the wind, thousands of grimy footprints, the wire fencing a mere indication that "it was once green here." A massive force raged through the squares during the day, clashing against every bench, every statue, every plant. But after midnight, it was as if the catastrophe was deep in the past. Despite the fury of the day, once quiet, the bushes and the trees appeared as if they could survive anything. In the darkness, they seemed to converse silently with each other, prisoners in a utilitarian architecture that was little more than an inflexible boundary in the shadows.

Whenever the wind ceased, I remained still as the trees, drinking in little sips, lost beyond time, until dawn when the first buses of the day broke the spell. I always emerged from those nights in an uneasy mood.

In contrast, when the wind roared at night, unleashing a game of opposites between the solid tree trunks and the pliable branches, I would feel invigorated and start pacing around, trying to capture every angle of this dance, observing how they resisted or gave in.

A relative finally found me and convinced me to stay with him. Soon after that, Aron attacked Eligia.

Four years earlier, when I was eighteen and had begun to drink regularly, it became apparent to me just how ridiculous our propensity toward evil can be. It was particularly obvious in bars: pathetic drunks getting into fights, anxiously revealing their perversions, sabotaging what little good remained in their lives. The outcome was always impressive and laughable. Among people who knew how to bear existence sober and carry out their ambitions, this propensity toward evil seemed counterproductive.

These were days when history was systematically making clowns of us all. There was political instability, and the news consisted of an endless parade of soldiers and civilians with political paraphernalia, promising rewards or punishments left and right. After a few years or even months, these parades would disappear having accomplished nothing. Some of the "saviors" would reemerge after their fall from power; and we would see them in the flesh, at a bar or nightclub, their dull eyes lighting up only when they got a chance to reminisce about their glory days.

And that is how, from an early age, my idea of evil became that of a joke.

On one occasion, a lawyer came to the clinic with a folder belonging to Aron and all the documents we would need to inherit his estate. He held each document to Eligia's eyes and explained the contents in a monotone voice. Among the papers—which included deeds of all the divorce proceedings they had initiated over their twenty-eight years of marriage—we found a photo of Eligia leaning comfortably on Aron's shoulder. I didn't reflect on her expression of happiness in the photo or the reason why Aron had decided to keep it. I snatched it and put it in my pocket, assuming this would be the last thing she'd want to see.

Later, at a bar, I examined the image. I understood their relationship was complicated and did not easily lend itself to words. The episode made me question my assumptions, but I had no patience for subtlety, and, luckily for me, the scaffolding of needs and tasks built around Eligia's suffering was enough to keep me from diving too deep. The idea that chaos is more bearable than a desert void—which I had constantly imagined in thinking about Aron's spirit and Eligia's body—was sowed in me at this time: the thought that evil is beyond willpower, that, once it affects the mind (and this happens less frequently than assumed), it operates as it does in nature, involuntarily, absolutely, in an absent manner, as in the desert.

To distract Eligia during those brief moments of full consciousness, I got in the habit of reading her entertaining articles from a history magazine. One time, as I was paging through an issue, I found an article about political resistance against fascism in the 1930s. I saw Aron's photo. The text was a transcript of a speech he had given in 1934:

THE TIME TO FIGHT HAS COME!

From every corner of our motherland, from universities to factories, we have heard the clamor of the new generation that refuses to remain silent in the face of arrogant oligarchic minorities that threaten to undermine the democratic and republican foundations of this nation.

An intense crisis has shaken our community over the past three years. We have seen a breakdown of constitutional integrity and the perversion of judicial norms; there is little dignity left in government. We have been humiliated on the world stage; our rights have been mutilated, our foreign credit curtailed, the honor of our army dragged through the mud. And today we see the complete impunity of armed groups imbued with a plagiarized ideology that no longer hides its contempt for democracy and announces the imposition by force of a class dictatorship. The conservative right fights for the advent of this dictatorship, because it knows it is the only way of maintaining its monstrous political and economic privileges, which embarrass and impoverish the country.

The wave of violence shaking civilization, with its hatred of other races and borders, can have no place among us.

The right is preparing the definitive subjection of the will of the people as enshrined in the Constitution, the brutal slavery of the working class, and the surrender of our national resources to foreign imperialism and capitalism.

Faced with this humiliating spectacle, we created the Democratic Alliance, an organization of civil struggle that draws its inspiration from the most basic principles of the Constitution ...

With this manifesto we exhort all Argentines of courage to act. We repudiate weakness and inaction, and call on every man who is young of heart, body, and mind, without regard to class or creed.

We are fully cognizant of the implications of our words, and assume full responsibility. We pledge our honor and life to this struggle.

—Aron Gageac

The article also chronicled the many times Aron was imprisoned, his escapes, his conspiracies against the military governments, his exiles and hunger strikes, the trains he would hire to mobilize his supporters, his underground newspapers ... A feeling of contradiction returned to me. Sure, the old man had been violent and cruel, but he had also done everything with passion, risked everything for his ideals, and spent entire fortunes to fight dictators, after squandering others on European whores. I didn't mention the article to Eligia.

One morning, the door opened, and I caught a curious person peering into the room from the hallway. He stared as if from a different world, from another reality where health and sickness were united in one word—"normal." That world in which one has a right to stare in fear at what is simply unnatural.

A normal man comes to visit a normal patient, someone suffering pain no one wished upon them. Later that day, I saw this man telling his relatives: —The poor woman! How can they keep her like that! —he raised his arms to illustrate her crucified immobility. The whole group watched him, quickly forgetting about their own patient, hissing with difficulty through a tracheotomy.

I spent my free time at the bar, and that was the extent of my contact with the outside world. Tending to Eligia was tolerable, because we both liked silence. There were never any dramatic scenes or tantrums; she went hours in complete silence, not giving the slightest indication of what she was thinking. I was only disturbed by the moments when proximity was unavoidable: helping her sit up, which made the hidden wounds of her body partially visible, helping her drink and eat, washing her skin.

This is how the truth chips away at our ingenuity, our protective scaffolding.

After three months, Eligia's only identifiable feature was her short nose, which had petrified along with the concave cheeks. A quiet, icy fury clustered around that old feature, the archeology of her former self. It was the final letter of an identity that was leaving her, lashed by the waves of a new, inhuman profile. The fins had disappeared quickly, but the back of the nose, supported by cartilage, resisted for some time. On the last surgery, they had removed the tip of the nose and the soft part of the cartilage, so the last bulwark that made her recognizable was gone.

In the fourth month of treatment, seeing Eligia's face produced in me a feeling of freedom. The end of functionalism: if we are what we are due to our current form, then Eligia had surpassed us. It is true, however, that a face, a body, mean so much to us that their presence is always vague, blurred by the turmoil of things manifesting in their naked totality. Faces—at least for a shy person like myself—only become precise in the act of recollection.

One day the new head of the medical team arrived. No one explained to us why the previous doctor had left. His replacement announced with forced jubilation that the first stage was over. He praised Eligia for her courage, for being an excellent patient, so stoic, as strong a woman as he had seldom seen in his life. It was time for well-deserved rest and recuperation, before starting reconstructive surgery, "which worked wonders." He also praised the work of the previous doctor, "a wise man despite his unorthodox ideas about 'symbolic efficacy,' but that never interfered with his scientific work, believe me."

—We have limited experience with cases like yours—he continued. I recommend working with Dr. Calcaterra, in Milan. He is the best in the field. In fact, he was already a pioneer in facial reconstructive surgery before the war. You can imagine his level of experience. It is true that my colleague disagrees with Calcaterra on some things; one could almost say they approach surgery from two opposite perspectives. One specializes in burns, the other in reconstruction.

—What about a plastic surgeon?

—Facial reconstruction surgeons are the crème de la crème of plastic surgery. *We* act like the firefighters, trying to stop the damage so healing can begin. But they are the speleologists, the ones that can really go deep.

Before we left for Italy, a friend in the medical profession told me that no plastic surgeon in the country wanted to take Eligia's case because she was a well-known figure, and, no matter how hard they tried, the results weren't going to be pretty. "The clinic did what any burn unit would have done in a case like this: remove the necrosis and cover."

—What about the baths four times a day and the exposure to the moonlight, all useless?

—No. It served a purpose: to make you feel useful.

—

Montevideo, October 2, 1955

ESSAY: "I AM PROUD OF MY SCHOOL"
by Mario Gageac

In my third year at our beloved Herder German School, I would like to use this Essay as an opportunity to express my appreciation.

I remember the first day of class in 1953, when I arrived with my French-sounding last name and the little bit of German I had learned as a six-year-old boy, in Switzerland, and later practiced with a governess that spoke German though she was Polish. Before I came to this school, my German was almost forgotten. I had a lot of difficulty learning again, because this school is for boys who were born speaking this language, not strangers like me. I apologize for my mistakes.

At that time of arrival, I still felt fear, because eight months earlier, back in my country, I had been in the women's prison for a week, with my mother Eligia and my little sister, locked up, because the Police didn't want to say that Eligia was detained. I think the one who should have been in that Prison was the most powerful woman of my Country, the General's Wife, instead of us. She would have slept among the whores and thieves like us, because in that place they didn't even have a special place for political women. My country has not been through the Enlightenment: only the Middle Ages and Romanticism. Not like this Uruguayan land of freedom where we took refuge. I know I must not speak about these things: about my country, not a word.

But one of those dirty Whores wasn't good enough to be a follower of the General (that is why those women stayed in prison in those times, not too far in the past, after they had got around and were trying to be vice presidents, they treated me with much love and hugged me when they took Eligia to interrogation, and also the thief, she defended me, the one that yelled "Oligarch" when she saw me, and swore she would kill my entire family, including my grandfather).

When Eligia returned from interrogation, she energetically recommended that I shouldn't talk about national politics, and much less about the General and his Wife. That this was very dangerous. That if I said something wrong or a proper name, in prison we would stay forever. In short, about my country, absolutely nothing could be said. That was the best thing to do. I was not to talk.

I was also not to use words such as "Whore," which I am writing here, but I am confident that you, dear teacher, will understand very well how bad women are, and the one that was good to me I did not trust because she must have been hiding something in her mind.

When we escaped the dictatorship of my country, I landed in this small country and this great school, at the end of primary school.

That year of 1953, in the Herder, we did not have the secondary school yet. Only in 1954 our dear Herder School for Learning opened, long after the unjust closure during the World War. Every year, a new grade we inaugurated, so that I was always among the Older Kids. I like being in the grade of the Older Kids. That is how I understood—just as Headmaster von Zharschewsky told us and also our dear teacher Mr. Bormann—that it was a responsibility, unlike in church schools, that we should not beat the defenseless youngsters. Here, luckily, the only ones with the right to apply physical corrections are the teachers and the guards, not the older students, and they always do it with justice.

With the first punishments with the stick (which my friends later told me wouldn't hurt too much, although the first time it was done to me, I cried, like a little wimp), I understood that I had entered a reality that was entirely different from that of all the schools where I had studied in the past. I had gone through the other schools without building character, except for the first school in Freiburg in Switzerland, where the sisters kept beans or peas in their habits and made us kneel on the dry little balls, which they spread on the floor when we misbehaved. If we did something really bad, we also had to stare at the Sun.

Thanks to the advice of Detlef and Bernhardt, my best friends here in Montevideo (now both happy about their fatherland obtaining glorious victory at the World Cup, in which my country did not even want to participate, and Uruguay was eliminated because Hochberg was hurt and the Hungarians in overtime took advantage of the confusion and changed two players; I apologize for talking about banal topics), I understood that I had to adapt to a new spirituality and lucidity and adapt to a voluntary life path where all my actions conspired to achieve a superior Destiny.

Now that I am thirteen, I am convinced that my schools offered me the best education, without out-of-control private Emotions or feminine sentimentality. Here, in the boys section, failed school assignments end up being ripped to pieces by those who completed them wrong. They are destroyed in class in front of all your classmates, after the teacher explains why it was wrong. The first time it felt to me like an injury or a void, but with the passage of time (and thanks to my dear teachers who have much dedication to their work and returned after the school closure during the World War, and took up their Duty in this sad time after the war, which is a prewar with the Russians, but then the Russians will need us), I hear every time with more frequency: "Mr. Gageac, you have a good one," or "Distinguished," or "Outstanding!" and my chest full of Ideals expands. Only the teaching of Latin, as Eligia notes, is neglected here. But our headmaster says it is no longer practical.

The person who most praises me is the old drawing teacher, Mr. Bormann, even though I draw badly, but I listen to his explanations about great Art and Ideals attentively. It is said that this great wise man has been in Germany, and he says that he cares more about Ideals than Drawings. We must arrive to Ideals through observation, says Mr. Bormann: Laws of Physical Vision must be understood within the framework of the Canons and the Golden Mean. And he explains to us with prints the harmony of the classical statues. That is how my favorite teacher Mr. Bormann thinks. In addition, he is the most concerned about me in this boarding school, and treats me as if I were always lacking something.

Thanks to these friends, teachers, and Ideals, I feel a confidence in myself that I had not felt in my country and in the other countries where my father Aron moved with us. Confidence beyond the risks that the world puts before me, and all the doubts that exasperated me when I was a Child.

Now I have to return with my parents to my country, because the tyrant General has been deposed, and I will return on a Cruise! I am certain that I will no longer express emotions about every change in my home, city, country, and the social class of my father Aron. I am not sure I will feel as safe as I feel here. But when you can get an Outstanding for reciting Goethe, you cannot feel scared by what is happening in South America.

But before my departure, our beloved Headmaster von Zharschewsky died. His obituary was assigned to me to write for the school newspaper. I went by myself to the Office of the Headmaster, and saw his photos from the war. He was in uniform. I sat at the typewriter: "We lost a very special being, who gave everything and asked for nothing back. He was one of those exceptional beings who instead of wasting smiles, offered us spartan knowledge and examples. I remember the many times I tried to keep my back as straight as his, but always ended up getting tired and started hunching. But he, who was eighty, was always erect. When we were in his presence, I felt intimidated by his spiritual fortitude and wanted to be like him. Now, when I raise my eyes to see him in Heaven, I remember the Goethe verses we read in Class: "... die Beschwörung war vollbracht. / Und auf die gelernte Weise / Grub ich nach dem alten Schatze / Auf dem angezeigten Platze: / Schwartz und stürmisch war die Nacht." Which in Spanish means (do I dare translate?) ...

II

ELIGIA SPENT THE FOLLOWING summer and winter in the mountains, recovering in the company of my younger sister. I stayed in the capital, in Aron's apartment, after the judge ordered the removal of the yellow tape. There were still marks on the front door, which had been forced open by the police.

I returned with the few clothes I had, and made sure to leave everything as I had found it. My favorite room was the library, where I am trying to write as much as possible before the place is sold. At that time there was enough material to keep one entertained for many years: kitsch French pornography from the 1920s in lavish bindings with pseudohistorical drawings depicting Babylon and Alexandria; three decades' worth of underground antifascist newspapers that Aron himself had run against the dictatorships; more works by Stirner, Papini, and Lenin; autographed copies of terrible books authored by important politicians; and also the usual stuff of pretentious bookshelves, including the great philosophers, the French novelists of the nineteenth century, and works that had been given to Aron as gifts or that he had purchased because he found the titles attractive. Together, they all showed Aron's contradictions, which allowed each person that met him to form whatever image of the man they preferred.

Back then the walls of the room were covered with books (some were bottles of liquor that looked like book spines), and there was a Chinese-style desk with feet that looked like golden hooves. The wood was lacquered with warm black and cherry tones, further emphasized by the light-colored Persian rug with a pattern of flowers.

Here is where Aron threw the acid. Not a single drop fell on the desk; a black stain was visible on the carpet—enough to ruin it beyond repair, marking a trail that connected the desk with the Louis XVI–style chair where Eligia had been sitting during the meeting with the lawyers (though she was already getting up when the liquid hit her). The arms and legs of the chair remained untouched, but the acid had devoured most of the silk; gutting it, leaving the interlinings and frame fully exposed. The back seat cushion showed the scorched feathers of Eligia's breast.

There is a glass door on the western wall that opens onto a balcony. Once upon a time, it overflowed with ivy and jasmine. I remember afternoons when the sunlight would outline their shadows as it filtered into the room. On the corner of that same wall, on a small simple table, rests a surprisingly large chest, also with Chinese-style motifs. I had never looked inside, as it was always locked during the four years that I lived in the place, but I became curious after the suicide. I forced the lock, and to this day I can still see the clumsy scrapes that ruined the lacquer. In there, Aron had kept some pornographic photos that I managed to sell at a good price, and notebooks and report cards from our school years. I saw folders from some of the eight schools I attended. On a report card from my first Swiss school, Aron had written his plans regarding my studies; they included piano and Latin (which he did not know) and even fencing and prestidigitation lessons. In another folder, I found assignments from my humble little school in the mountains. I opened it at random and found a composition, "The Puma," on which Aron had crossed out my expression "paws with long nails" and written "claws"; on the margin he wrote in big letters "same for wild boar!" The comments must have been written several years later, seeing that he wasn't living with us at the time. I hated seeing his words of contempt, even fourteen years after the fact. I didn't continue digging through the school folders, but I did see one belonging to my years at the Herder School in Montevideo.

That's the room I chose for reading in my spare time during those final days of 1964. But a week after my return, the burns and scrapes on the furniture began to bother me, much like the specks of dry blood on the hospital bed sheets. I decided to do my reading in the small bedroom I had used for the past four years. The larger bedroom, which received better sunlight, no longer had a bed—it was removed after they found Aron dead on it. One of the glass windows was still broken. The bullet had lost momentum after ripping through his skull twice at the temples. Upon leaving his head, it pierced the curtain and the glass before finally bouncing off the closed shutters and falling to the ground. It had failed to escape the eighth floor and fly high above the gardens until reaching the dome of the church where the sun sets. I had thought those bullets were more powerful.

Years later, when I reviewed the court file for the suicide, I saw the forensic photos: Aron sitting in bed, wearing a camel robe with black, silk frogging. One hand held a whiskey, the other the .38 Long.

That summer I fell in love. It lasted through winter, a long parenthesis where I got to think about someone other than Eligia. The woman was beautiful, and at first I didn't feel like leaving for Italy. Luckily, this woman who had enthralled me wasn't the type to ask a man not to leave, and in the end it wasn't terribly hard to pack my suitcase and take out my old black coat—a tent of a thing where no stain or bulge was visible.

The last time I had traveled with Eligia was in 1952. Our plans didn't quite work out that time. My sister wasn't walking yet, and I was ten years old. We were on our way to Montevideo to meet Aron for one of their reconciliations, but the state police arrived just as the ship was about to depart. Eligia refused to disembark, claiming that as long as she was on board, she enjoyed "extraterritoriality." The captain begged her to come down, as every hour of delay cost him thousands of dollars in port fines. They were still arguing hours later when the police finally had enough and simply came on board, took her by the arm (she was still carrying her little daughter), and escorted us out. They took us to the women's prison, and we ended up staying there for a week. At the time, there were few women involved in politics, so women's prisons didn't have special wings for political prisoners. We were placed with the general population. After a few days, the police took my sister and me to a hotel and phoned our maternal grandmother to come get us. Eligia remained detained for a few months. Eventually, we traveled to Montevideo in secret.

Before attempting my second trip with Eligia—this time to Italy, in September of 1965—I had the foresight to remove all the bottles of cheap cognac my new love and I had been drinking. We lined them up along the stairway. I smiled. At the time, alcohol still had a good reputation: Bogart drank with his blonde, and cowboy John Wayne drank straight from the bottle (the first time I tried to imitate him, I made the rookie mistake of replacing his signature Scotch with a bottle of cheap grappa and nearly lost my soul in the attempt).

Eligia arrived from the mountains in a domestic propeller aircraft. The plane for our international flight was very tapered. The first jets recalled futuristic travels, interplanetary journeys, but truth be told they crashed more frequently than good old reliable planes. In the cabin, a boy of about eight started crying when Eligia came in. He was clearly too old for all that whining, but didn't seem to feel any shame. His mother did nothing to stop him, and the other passengers did their best to disappear behind a wall of silence. —What is it? What is it?! —asked the boy, to which the mother replied: —Don't stare, don't stare. Two minutes later the captain walked in. I thought of the time the ship captain asked us to get off the boat, and Eligia, stubborn as always, had refused.

The captain was all smiles and invited us to sit in first class. The seats were more comfortable, and they treated us like royalty. Prior to taking off, a stewardess, who was taller than the one in coach, asked if we wanted something to drink. I asked for whiskey and she brought me Scotch—a generous pour, and free. I hadn't had anything imported since my time with Aron. This one was definitely lighter than what he used to drink. Once in the air, they served us dinner with French wine and cognac. We were flying away from the sun, and I watched it sink into the ocean. After dinner, the stewardess started her performance: while a voice on the loudspeaker announced that we would be flying mostly over the ocean, and explained the location of the life jackets and how to put them on, this tall brunette acted out the instructions almost specifically for Eligia and me. The voice coming from the loudspeaker spoke in incomprehensible English over the static and ended with a reminder to adjust our clocks; behind these electric distortions, the voice actually sounded quite happy.

Eligia took her sleeping pill, but I chose to remain awake, excited about the idea of visiting the whiskey cart that the long-legged stewardess had parked at the end of the aisle. I awaited anxiously as she continued her presentation, smiling at me as she went over each step, placing the oxygen mask over her mouth and pulling the elastic band slowly so I knew exactly how to activate it.

When the show was over, I asked for another whiskey. She poured some more and sat two rows behind me. The cabin was blue, purple, and beige. You felt protected and comfortable there, breathing reheated air in this flying fish, while the ocean below turned to molten metal under the moonlight. I glanced back several times. The stewardess smiled. We wouldn't be able to talk if I stayed sitting next to Eligia, but I decided to stay put and look back every now and then. After a while she stopped smiling and began to look concerned. Finally, she came and, very professionally, asked in a low voice if I needed something. I requested another whiskey. This time she was almost too generous. This repeated a few times. I began to notice she was wearing a lot of makeup, also with beige, blue, and purple tones. I asked if the airline forced her to use their colors, or if it was her preference to be in harmony with this capsule shooting across the sky and no one really knowing if it was going to explode in midair.

—You're kind of weird, no? —she said with a frown.

At that time, flying to Rome took almost thirty hours. By the fourth whiskey, the moon had disappeared, the ocean had turned to black, and the red lights under the wing of the aircraft marked my only coordinates in space. The stewardess adopted an almost maternal air toward me, a bit complicit and ironic. —I understand —she said sweetly now, and looked at Eligia who was sleeping next to me. She brought me a juice glass filled with whiskey, then sat six rows back, put on an eye mask, and went to sleep.

I let my mind wander. I tried to imagine the nurses at the Italian clinic. One would look like Catherine Spaak. There would also be good art in Milan. After a few weeks, Eligia's skin would begin to look smoother and, thanks to the magic hands of the best reconstructive surgeon in the world, it would regain its rose color. There would be a few scars, but she would be a new woman. I caressed her; not her hand, but the sleeve of her brown dress. Eligia had always been very discreet with the colors of her wardrobe; she wanted to be seen as the intellectual that she was, a politician and an educator, efficient and modern, an image that was fully supported by her accomplishments: a gold medal in the faculty, a history professorship, advanced studies in Switzerland; twenty years in the field, she was one of the top-ranking members of her profession, and had sanctioned the Statute of Teachers, liberating thousands of female teachers from favoritism and the dangerous clutches of womanizing deputies. She was very proud of her accomplishments: day-care programs that allowed mothers to work, schools for technical training, educational reforms that created hundreds of schools in remote areas, the modernization of pedagogy to embody true democratic values. Deep down, in her naive, technocratic soul, she had seen herself—during her time as a civil servant—continuing the work of the famous politician who was married to the General, a woman who was her exact opposite in method and style. Eligia had hoped to show that empowered with a rational education, the women of her country could rise to the challenges of the modern world.

Although she had ended up in prison several times thanks to her enemy, the General's wife, Eligia still felt a certain admiration for her, though she would never have dared compete with her energetic style. She believed it was enough to study and to be efficient.

Twelve years after her last stint in prison, she now traveled east to recover a semblance of her face so she could appear in public again. She dreamed of the future with her mouth open and the "urgent" skin grafts barely covering her bones, while a child's voice repeated in her ear "What is it? What is it?" The embalmed corpse of the General's wife—who died the same year we escaped to Montevideo—had mysteriously disappeared after the revolution that overthrew the power couple in 1955.

My thoughts returned to the golden bottles in the cart. I tiptoed to the end of the aisle where the stewardess had tucked it away. It was dark and I couldn't find the whiskey, so I ended up drinking a sweet-tasting liquor from another bottle. Bottle and glass in hand, I turned around and was suddenly face-to-face with a feminine figure. She was shorter than the stewardess, and I could barely see her face.

—Eligia! ... The bathroom is the other way. You scared me.

—Don't be scared, I'm not your mother —said the stewardess. She wasn't wearing her high heels. —You should have woken me up; that's what I'm here for, to assist you ... Did you pour that much? Is it always like this, or only when you're flying? ... Would you like more? Perhaps some food? Whatever you like ... Just tell me what the hell you want.

—Yes, I'd like some more—I said.

—Men under thirty always travel in search of their mothers or to escape from them. You are the only one I've seen actually traveling with her. And I've been doing this for years ...

—Women should be more self-confident, instead of painting their faces like clowns. Why do you wear so much makeup?

—Do you have a girlfriend?

—Not quite.

—Why not?

—What do I know. I guess I didn't have good role models. Don't ask me complicated questions ... I don't feel well.

—That's because you drank too much without food in your stomach. I can fix you something, perhaps some cold cuts. It will make you feel better.

The plate she brought was overflowing with meat. I placed it on top of the drinks cart and tried to cut some, but the blunt metal cutlery made it impossible. The stewardess returned to the main cabin and retrieved something from her purse. She came back with a yellowish object.

—Here, try with this.

—What is it?

—I bought it in a flea market, I forget where. I use it to shave, but it's too sharp and ends up cutting me. But it will work for this.

I stared at the object: it looked like a naked female body, no more than fifteen centimeters. A metal rim protruded from the center, near the hip. I flicked the blade open in the dark. The meat posed no resistance.

A few days later, at the clinic in Milan, I would study the object in detail during the long hours of waiting. The knife was made of hardened paste, from a mold; nothing too artistic. It was shaped like a fish with a woman superimposed, her head close to the fish's mouth and her feet resting on the bolt holding the blade. Her human features were more evident than the animal's; they prevailed with protuberant bulges and exaggerated curves. The effect was involuntary, the result of a poor mold and finish.

—Come, I'll take you back to your seat —said the stewardess when she saw I had stopped eating. She poured me another drink. She was in her fifties and probably no longer able to fly in the major airlines. I couldn't tell if she was trying to comfort or seduce me; she took me by the hand, not the arm. We walked down the aisle and passed the row where Eligia lay dreaming. My legs began to feel stiff. A dark heaviness filled the cabin. I felt my steps slow down.

—I have to take care of her —I said to my guide, coming to a stop.

—You have to take care of yourself.

I finished my drink on my seat and slept all the way to Dakar.

... Do I dare?: "... The exorcism is complete./ And I've learned the way./ Searched for ancient treasures / In the indicated places: / Black and turbulent was the night."

When I finished translating these verses, I saw myself standing inside the pit that awaited von Zharschewsky. I raised my eyes again to the sky, waiting for inspiration, a good translation, but the only thing that came to mind were the lyrics to a song that was popular then: "We will see him sad and bitter, / we will see him sad and without love, / we will see him sad and bitter / because the girl next to him / said no ... " I tried to think of other things, sentences with more interesting words, like Abode, Journey, Snowfall, Return.

I stood inside the pit. The other headstones were at eye level with my thirteen-year-old self. I was holding the obituary that I had written. The bottom of the pit was damp. I was surrounded by violet mud that smelled of woman and limestone, and I felt at peace, resigned to the fact that I was sinking. The mud covered my eyes; I was drowning in a viscous swamp. When I surfaced again, I emerged into a mire with no end in sight, surrounded by a blinding light because the day of the burial for fucking von Zharschewsky was rainy, yet bright and overcast. I was floating in the mud, not knowing which way to go when, suddenly, a rowboat passed me. The only passenger was von Zharschewsky, who was dressed in work clothes, leaning on the far side while staring at me. There was a white marble cross on the side of the boat that had my photograph on the center. On the arms, my name was inscribed along with the following line: "In this fucking country, you never know who you are." Von Zharschewsky smiled like I had never seen before: an open smile, cheerful and vital. It was the smile of a carefree man.

The mud sucked me in again. When I was fully submerged and thinking I was about to disintegrate, I suddenly found myself flying high across the sky; I was blond and taller than I would ever be. A reddish drizzle made it difficult to breathe. I saw a black stain on the ground and headed toward it. I descended on an enormous nest of black ants with very long legs that curled like hair. I heard a voice say: "Be careful not to step on them!"—so I started eating them; and the more I ate, the lighter I felt. Finally, I found the only entrance to the nest. Poking around with my fingers, I tried to extract more ants, but they were all outside. I started flying again, this time against my will, rising through the drizzle which was now deep purple.

—

When I woke up in Dakar, the stewardess was chatting with the new crew. There were two substitutes, and my friend pointed me out with her finger and gave a quick nod. I returned the greeting.

I went out into the airport. That day I had my vodka debut: returning to the plane, I asked one of the new stewardesses for a screwdriver. These two were younger than the previous one. She brought me a glass filled to the rim. I assumed the woman from the night before had asked the new crew to be generous with me. I thought of her with fondness, certain that I would never see her again. A wave of affectionate feelings came over me, and I clutched the knife she gave me as if it were a talisman.

Leaving Dakar, I was a bit confused with the time zones, and the sudden appearance of daylight hurt my eyes. Two more passengers had come on board, ending the intimacy of the night before. In her sleep, Eligia had settled into an awkward position, and due to her retracted jaw, she started making moist, guttural, strenuous sounds. That would be my lullaby for the next two years. I tried to adjust her head gently but it fell back in the same position. I decided to wake her. Time for breakfast! I said. The rest of the flight was a delight. The girls spoiled me with everything I wanted, under Eligia's silent gaze.

As we flew over Rome in the twilight, I leaned over to peek through the window. I had been to Italy in 1949, when I was seven, and in 1958, when I was sixteen. These childhood memories had a hierarchy of their own: I remember a saint's mummy in an urn, but not Michelangelo's *Moses*. I remember seeing armor with a trimmed helmet to accommodate the owner's mustache, but not the Galleria Borghese. I could not distinguish between my recollection of those tours and the black-and-white, or sepia, illustrations that good old Mr. Bormann used for his art lectures in Montevideo. That combination of memories from my childhood and adolescence created an "aesthetic corner" of the worst kind, a place of Virgins from the early Renaissance, gold gilding, and that kind of thing. I stared at Italy greedily, and asked for another screwdriver.

On the ground, the plane shut down its engine with a sigh of relief. Eligia and I were both light travelers, so we quickly made to the exit while the others hurried to get all their suitcases, bags, and presents. As we were about to step out, one of the stewardesses stopped us. —Please, you have to wait until everyone else gets out. Intrigued, Eligia and I looked at each other and took the seats closest to the door while the other passengers deplaned.

After a long wait, the other stewardess and the copilot—who didn't even greet us—also got off. Only then did the stewardess, who had been standing next to us with a forced smile, say we could leave the plane. Numb from so much sitting, Eligia leaned on me. She walked with difficulty, but the cool air of autumn felt good. An ambulance was parked at the foot of the stairway. I thought this kind of attention from the captain was a bit too much; after all, the small political party of which Eligia was an acting member wasn't even part of the current government. Three big men brought a wheelchair up the steps and invited Eligia to sit. She refused at first, but the stewardess asked her to comply: —These are the rules. If you fall or hurt yourself, it will be my fault. So please, ma'am! The men carried Eligia in the chair like some kind of idol. I sensed a reverential, astonished fear in their effort. Curious people began to gather at the base of the stairway—airport employees, passengers from other flights—all staring in disbelief as the chair descended in a continuous movement, almost as if it were floating. I studied the bystanders: people with toned arms and legs and fleshy faces—I found them incredible, enviable... All this fanfare struck me as ostentatious. The stewardess remained by our side as we descended the steps. I remembered the time the police escorted us down the ramp of the ship. I thought I was going to faint.

As soon as we touched ground, a male nurse came out of an ambulance and invited me to climb in the back. Another nurse and a guard were waiting for me inside. They asked me not to make a scene, and I told them off. Next thing I knew, they were injecting me with who knows what as the male nurse explained:

—These are my orders. You can't go to customs this drunk. Please understand it's for your own good.

Then he left, but the guard stayed on. I told him I felt perfectly fine, that my travel companion had been left outside in a wheelchair.

—You have to wait half an hour—the man replied curtly, and I understood that insisting more would end up with a trip to the security office.

After half an hour, I was released from the ambulance. The sun was setting, and around the aircraft, mechanics conducted their routine maintenance on every surface and opening in the machine, like a lady and her servants at her toilette. I could see the engines and the metallic interiors; men in multicolor uniforms connected cables and pipes to strange blowing machines with blinking manometers. The effect was a precise mechanical process where even the smallest drop of excess oil was wiped before it could stain the cement ground. In the most convenient places, small black-and-yellow carts connected easily with the entrails of the machine.

Eligia was waiting for me in her wheelchair; she'd been abandoned on the track by the side of the plane. In the cabin above, everything was dark. The young stewardess had left. Eligia looked at me, but couldn't form any expression. That's the only reason she decided to speak.

—Mario ... please don't drink like Aron.

—Don't compare me to that savage! —I said. —Look at what he did to you. I'm the exact opposite of that.

During the night flight to Milan, I thought of the stewardess from the previous night. I remembered how she pointed me out to her replacements at the end of her shift. That is where her betrayal started, and how I ended up in that ambulance. Around her razor, I tightened my grip.

III

> Soft like her cheek it quivers
> Flowing glances that recognize limits
> and her body is a mixture of woods,
> hair and nocturnal fears.
>
> —Raúl Santana

WE STAYED AT THE clinic where Professor Calcaterra would be operating. The facility was located in the south of the city, on Via Quadronno, a small street lined with postwar buildings that looked like emergency urban surgery to mitigate the destruction of bombs. We approached through Corso di Porta Vigentina, driving along a sad wall that had been erected to hide the debris. When the taxi turned on the corner of Quadronno, I saw a small bar. We arrived at the clinic after ten at night and asked for the smallest room and a discount for our prolonged stay. The next morning, at the reception office, we confirmed what everyone in the family knew but no one had dared say: the cost of Eligia's surgeries was going to bankrupt us.

From the moment we stepped foot in the clinic, the staff showed a great level of knowledge and professionalism: not a single nurse or maid ever hesitated when performing a task, and no one seemed overly curious about Eligia's appearance. They made her feel she was in the right place.

The green door to our room was very wide, and had two panels, though one of them was more than large enough for the food and medical carts to go through. It led to an interior corridor lined with lockers of the type found in sports gyms. There was a small bathroom with no tub. Most patients at the clinic couldn't move on their own, so the facilities had been designed for the use of their companions. The room was laid out for maximum privacy. Even when the door was wide open, it was impossible to see the large bed from the corridor. The intimacy was sepulchral.

A large adjustable bed dominated the center of the room. It had a caster-wheel mechanism that the nurses could activate with their feet. A reproduction of *Mont Sainte-Victoire* faced the bed. Its brilliant colors prevented any aerial perspective. I covered the image with a towel, but, for the next twenty-four months, the maids would keep taking it down: "Bad man! Don't you see that the happy colors lift her spirits?" Professor Calcaterra, on the other hand, smiled when he saw the towel covering the image.

On that same wall, to the right of the motionless patient, was a tall, narrow window with an adjustable shutter system that allowed a partial view of the outside. A church, Santa Maria al Paraíso, covered the entire view.

To the left of the bed was the hidden vestibule that led to the entrance of the room, thus creating the sense that you were in some kind of theatrical stage, where visitors suddenly appeared from the wings. It would always come as a surprise unless you heard them first. On the same wall as the entrance, parallel to the bed, was a green plastic sofa bed for the patient's companion. When opened, the small cot barely reached the height of the cranks and levers raising or lowering the patient's bed's great contraption.

To the right of the bed was an adjustable table used to feed the patients without having to move them. The lousy design made it useless, as I later learned. The green floor of the room was plastic to facilitate the use of disinfectants . . . I hate plastic.

Eligia seemed hopeful. From the moment we entered the building that first night, I noticed her mood became lighter. The attitude of the staff, who acted normally around her wounds, soon had a narcotic effect, and she was able to relax. Her spirit retreated to a region far from her daily life, carefree, a space where her thoughts could turn toward hope without the burden of everyday sorrows. But with this abandonment of her carnal identity a great heaviness seemed to envelop her wounds, a greater density that intensified her cursed rocklike nature. While a new serenity gleamed from the depths of her eyes (which were difficult to appreciate behind the leaden chelonian eyelids), the rest of her face filled with a silent density that hadn't been visible at the other clinic, where she used to lean into the substance of her pain and grimace. This would check the progress of her transformations. Back in our country, her rocky surface possessed a lunar weightlessness, but in those early hours in Milan, the surface inverted, and instead of following the ascending trajectory of the acid, it turned into a substance that only wished to fall, to come off the bones that barely held it together. She seemed to want to crawl beyond the reach of any gaze, as in cahoots with the architects that planned for the privacy of the room, by designing a diagonal vestibule.

Thanks to the architecture of the place and the impersonal attitude of the staff, we basically lived like hermits. Our isolation was enhanced by a formalism disguised as humanitarian disposition. While the bodies were always busy with some task, the voices repeated the same few lines to exhaustion every day, like those pianists who travel the world playing the same few sonatas. One could hear "Good afternoon! Here's your meal, but we have to check your temperature first." It was obvious, from the first syllable, that they expected no response. It would have shocked them to hear something like: "There's no need to take my temperature. I feel perfectly fine. As to the meal, I would like to taste it first and, if I don't like it, to order something different, perhaps a chicken thigh with sage." A response like that would have been unimaginable, and although I imagined such words coming out of Eligia's mouth every time they brought the food, she was always silent, accepting every meal and verbal command without question.

The predictability that surrounded the patients, along with the interior design of the place, had a simple objective: to ensure no one felt entitled to express a preference or felt justified in complaining about the fact that they lay there completely destroyed.

If someone cried out during a routine procedure, the nurses seemed to take it almost as an insult: "Why are you doing this?

Don't you see everyone here wants to see you well and is doing their best to help you heal?" And if it seemed appropriate, they'd slip a joke about some other patient, perhaps the man who had lost both hands and would be taking a long vacation. The end was always the same: "And besides, think about your family, who loves you so much. What a shame if they saw you complaining like this!" By the end of the little lecture, the patient usually looked rather embarrassed.

This straightjacket imprisonment contained all the true inmates, the people who were there for the "long stay." After a month in these rooms, death presented itself as an insignificant alternative, as the body had already been abandoned by its owner to the asceticism and "smiling humanitarianism" of the medical staff. No extravagance, no unpredictable action was allowed.

Behind the discreet manners, one could perceive *the true limits*, hidden and firm: the security personnel on the ground floor and the deaf "disassembly line" working with formidable efficiency, disposing of corpses as necessary and quickly cleaning the room for the next visitor.

Eligia's situation eventually earned her some secondary benefits: there was an air of distinction around the long-term residents, who had been there fifteen or twenty days. This made them feel entitled to look down on those who weren't there for a reconstructive procedure, those who came for plastic surgery and would only stay for two days—their burden was vanity rather than a missing nose or mouth. By the time we completed our first year at the sanatorium, Eligia commanded an epic respect. But I'll be honest, the wall of "smiling humanitarianism" made me miss Aron.

To recall his image, my memory focused on his eyes, white

and intense, when he wanted to instill fear and show no mercy. The two spheres conjured the adjacent features—the eye sockets, the bridge of the nose. From there my mind quickly generated the nostrils, the cheekbones, the mouth ... until my deductive reconstruction was complete. Only then did I realize that the origin—the white spheres—had no gaze.

I undertook a supplementary search, not of visual memory, but a reconstruction of his intentions—the imprecise psychology that in those times also struck me as stupid—as an exercise to understand Aron's desire to penetrate flesh in any way, to violently possess everything within his reach, especially anything that tried to escape him or was about to disappear. I arrived, without wanting to, at the core of his panic: the presence of a vagina. For a brief second I felt compassion for this violent Don Juan. But then I remembered all the aggressions I had suffered from him and felt outraged. Here I was, an innocent who despised all violence. I declared myself a pacifist, not out of love for the kind of future that peace could bring me, but from a fearful familiarity with the violence that can be engendered in the corners of the soul.

What would he do in this sanitarium? Without doubt, he would fight everything, fix his attention on some unlucky nurse, complain about the room and the poor quality of the print on display—demand that a Cézanne be replaced with something pornographic or at least something from Goya—and start a scene on his first night, so everyone at the clinic would know that he, Aron Gageac, had arrived in his camelhair robe with black silk ... and was ready to take on anyone who contradicted him. A wave of sympathy rushed through my blood. I could not imagine him in a secondary role as a companion, or as a patient. In order to be admitted into this sanatorium, some kind of destruction had to befall the patient, but I couldn't imagine him with Eligia's wounds. He had almost no signs of deterioration when we saw him at the morgue. The body had been stored in one of the freezers. It looked rather healthy, as if some kind of indestructible element remained at its core: "He would have lived a thousand years," said the coroner, in front of his relatives, who had cherished hope that perhaps some cancer was the explanation for his final gesture. A band around the head concealed the perforations on his temples and kept the jaw attached to the rest of the skull.

From the morgue, we headed to the crematorium. The friend who was supposed to serve as a witness fainted, so we were forced to go in. "It's just a formality, you don't really have to look," said the graveyard clerk. But I could not help it: the Wagnerian stillness surrounded by flames, the darkening mass, and finally, the scorching farewell.

Aron's image was incompatible with this clinic. My wave of sympathy returned, but I repressed it at once. I was not going to allow myself this affinity. He had carefully planned his departure to cause the maximum damage. I will not let him in—is what I kept telling myself that night in Italy. I was going to rebuild myself with the same tenacity that defined Eligia, I was going to contradict Aron's designs. I was going to be the anti-Aron, and find my own way of being strong, my own way of challenging fate. My indifference would not be a filial debt.

—Don't fall back into the old habits. Try to sleep. We're both tired from the journey—Eligia said to me that first night in Milan.

The night nurse brought us something to eat and said the professor would visit the next morning. Eligia's meals were included in the clinic's fees, but I had to sign an extra voucher for a sandwich. Eligia and I considered the issue of my meals.

—Your food is included —I said. —I just need to find a small restaurant around here.

I promised myself I would find a cheap place to eat to lessen the expense and compensate for the mandatory drinks. I went to the bathroom to put on my pajamas, while Eligia changed in the room. We fell asleep right away, but I woke up in the middle of the night. I noticed that the room was never completely dark. The blinds always let in some of the light from Corso di Porta Vigentina and the church. The glow washed over the white cotton sheets covering Eligia. She was still. She looked so small. My blankets were green, but the sheets were white, like hers, and they also seemed to glow in the dark. As I propped myself up, I felt a warm moisture near my navel … I was indignant. I didn't remember the last time this had happened! What a surprise, especially after all the drinking during the flight. If I was going to bother drinking so much they would have to call an ambulance on me, I thought on that distant night, at least it should be guaranteed that disgusting incidents like this didn't happen. My pajama pants were wet, and the liquid had run down my left hip and into the bedsheets. Quivering in terror, I looked at Eligia. I imagined the next day when a nurse that looked like Catherine Spaak saw the stain. What humiliation. I blamed whatever they injected me with in that ambulance. It wasn't the first time alcohol landed me in an ambulance, and they had given me coramine before. I cursed the male nurse from the airport, and I cursed the stewardess who offered me all that whiskey, only to betray me.

Trying not to make a sound, I snuck into the vestibule and

took out a pen from my coat. I showered, washing the spot on the pajama pants; then I put the wet pants back on. Back in the sofa bed, I spilled the ink from the pen on the bedsheet. Then I paced around the room for a while, glancing every now and then at Eligia's bed. Finally, I lay down, careful to put the washed part of the pajama on the ink puddle. In the hours that remained until the room was cleaned, the water, ink, and semen would combine and form a stain that could easily be explained as someone falling asleep with a pen in hand. My body heat would surely hasten the process.

I never remembered the dream that caused it. Ten years later, I realized that I haven't remembered *any* dream since that night. The last dream before that was in the plane ... At the clinic I woke up with the confusing sensation of images fleeing me in a haze, but, as soon as I realized where I was, I turned to my cleaning chores and the fading memory was lost. During the next two years, I was frequently assailed by the same urge to grasp these images before they escaped me, but I always failed. On the bright side, I didn't wet my bed again for the rest my life.

But my strategy hadn't worked. The maid on the morning shift looked nothing like Catherine Spaak: she was blonde, with short, dull hair, approaching fifty, and somewhat overweight. I had left a few books next to my bed so the nature of the accident would seem all the more obvious. When I tried to explain what happened, she didn't even bother to reply. I wanted a *biombo*, I said—a folding screen—one of the Italian words that neorealist cinema had failed to teach me. To make myself understood, I resorted to hand gestures, which made me feel even more impotent. Finally, the woman, whose breath smelled like seasoned ham, replied—Ah! A room divider. But you don't want a *biombo*—she said, pronouncing the word in Spanish and laughing—or you won't be able to watch your mother. Would you be able to assist her during an emergency from behind a *biombo*? No, that's not how you care for a patient. I understand these things. It would be a different matter if you hired a nurse to be here during the night, so you could rest or even go out, dance, whatever... Then you could have a *biombo*."

The price for a special nurse was prohibitive. I imagined an unknown woman watching over us as I ejaculated on the sheets in my sleep. —Anyhow—she continued, seeing the look on my face—if not every night, perhaps a shift here and there; I have a cousin who specializes in the care of patients like her, you should see how she's able to handle them! You would think they were puppets stuffed with feathers; in her hands, they don't feel a thing, nothing. What she has is truly a gift! It's a talent you're either born with or not. You see, the most difficult thing with patients like her is moving her around for different things. Just feeding a patient like her is an art. Imagine how a single careless motion can ruin a skin graft; one tiny mistake and everything is lost. And then, the material—I assumed she was referring to the skin, not the gauze or cotton—soon expires. You must take good care of it. You don't know what mess you've gotten yourself into trying to do this alone. Come to the treatment room sometime, and check out the lifts and special baths that you need to know how to use in cases like this. But the idea of a woman, whose breath smelled of strong spices, moving Eligia like a puppet stuffed with feathers bothered me.

The maids and the nurses returned later in the morning to

clean the room. As soon as they finished, Professor Calcaterra came in. He was a healthy old man with a soothing voice, even when the meaning of his words was disturbing. His firm confidence immediately rubbed off on Eligia. The thought that this poor woman had no choice but to put her fate in the hands of doctors upset me. Professor Calcaterra's face was synthetic—the mouth, the nose, and the eyebrows all resolved in a single economic stroke—while his wide forehead and cheekbones extended to the small ears, the thinning white hair, and his prow-shaped jaw.

The professor was always surrounded by three or four assistants who usually kept quiet, but were ready to answer any questions. It looked like a capable team. The fees had already been settled via correspondence, and it was clear that Aron's depleted estate would not be enough.

—It will be a long healing process, very long —said Calcaterra—but I assure you that you will recover all your functions. The damage has been great, but there are solutions ... Take a look —he said, as his index finger traced the capricious paths formed by the ridges and scars. His finger moved steadily in one direction, but ended up describing circles duplicating those on her skin.

—Labyrinths, my dear madam, in which you yourself get lost. Useless inventions! Whims! Labyrinths! What could they mean? I have studied in depth the reports from my colleagues overseas and the photos ...

—The photos? What photos? —asked Eligia.

—Someone took photos in the operating room to track your progress. You don't remember? ... Perhaps during the anesthesia ... A great service to science.

And he focused on Eligia's face.

—Ah! It's a truly complex problem: a labyrinth in motion. He sighed with theatrical grief. —Some images should be reserved only for those with expert vision, those who dare to look into the unknown with a knowledge more profound than the confusion created by the acid, "a reconciling knowledge" as someone religious would say ... People should listen to them.

—But I assume that with everything you have seen in your many years of practice —I said, with a bit of irony in my voice— you already have that knowledge, that profound vision to interpret what is happening.

—No, I didn't acquire it through the medical profession. In this specialty, you must also be able to intuit something beyond the reach of science, beyond the hand, or the eye: the hidden movements of matter, the changes under the skin. There were cases where I sewed up a shoulder, and the stitches ended up emerging at the hip. Everything that enters our flesh is like a bottle in the sea. We don't know the currents, the forces at play. Where they come from, and why. We only see what happens at the surface. What lies beyond is inexplicable ... What is the skin concealing from us? There must be a fundamental lesson underneath, a reason why a surface so desired, worshipped, loved, can be transformed by fire or acid into such an astonishing landscape. It is not waste—understand?—it is not a collapse: it's a new construction removed from the will of the architect. You almost have to invent a new word for it, something like "the enigmatic constructive collapse." That is the only way to explain the portentous regeneration that will sometimes occur. There is a power beneath the surface! You will see how the stitches from the emergency treatment begin to reemerge like arrowheads returning from the past. What uncontrollable suffering! The flesh no longer knows what to do with itself, it has lost its north, its meaning. It is not strange that what is inside of her wants to get out. Madam, do you know what our strategy will be? We will challenge the whirlwind, the ordered abyss. On the surface, on the skin, you will find only superficial solutions, the stuff of emergency surgery. But we who reconstruct, we work in the depths. Instead of covering, we're going to dig in, to go where the acid was not able to reach. For now, the labyrinth spans over half your skin, there is no exit. So we must dig! It is the only way to solve this. Madam, you have been "vitriolized." Vitriol, you understand ... —he recited some Latinisms I couldn't decipher, but they sparked a glimmer of hope and respect in Eligia's eyes.

The doctor glanced at me and noticed my bewilderment.

—We will do away with all this confusion. The burnt flesh is part of a larger muscular structure, very complex and wise. The previous doctors removed what was obviously damaged, but they left the parts of the structure that weren't burned. A useless scaffold. An incomplete structure is chaos, or even worse, a failure of reason, ruins in which everything is lost. We will add new matter, but we will erect it on a healthy foundation, a firm and clear base —he said, almost in a whisper. His words had a calming effect on Eligia, but to me they invoked a new overwhelming series of colors and shapes; I wondered how long it would take to reach that firm and clear foundation.

—Madam, we will dig in search of the Creator, we will look for Him in the depths of your wounds. We will search and, when we find Him, we will ask Him to make you a new woman. And so, from the hatred that sought to destroy you, from that cursed acid, from those wounds, you, Madam, you will find your great truth, where you will be able to build again, this time forever. Madam, do you know what the symbol of vitriol is in alchemy? You will be surprised. It is Cupid! The ardent love that punctures and regenerates. But it is not a capricious symbol. Like love, the flaying of a burn has a rational side: to discover interior beauty ... You, young man, who have time, go admire the statue of St. Bartholomew in our Duomo, a saint so transparent.

The old man said these words with dignity and conviction. I found them excessive, but they had the desired effect on Eligia.

—We can start tomorrow. There's no time to waste—concluded the professor.

He gave some instructions to his assistants and nurses, and disappeared behind a cloud of white coats and respect.

We cancelled our plans to go to Brera that afternoon. Eligia had to stay in bed and keep a strict diet. She sent me to buy some small things, anticipating a period of immobility and not wanting to be taken by surprise.

While running the errands, I only got a brief glimpse of the Milanese autumn. As soon as I returned, they brought Eligia a simple lunch; then, after a visit from one of the professor's assistants, they gave her some pills without any explanation.

I went to the corridor. A group of young women had gathered by the nurses' office and greeted me with smiles. They were talking about plastic surgery, and praising Professor Calcaterra.

—I don't care if it costs a fortune. It's for the rest of your life and the professor is the best; he inspires so much confidence! Also, he explained in great detail everything he would do. Did you know that the nose is just a structure? When it is not in harmony, it must be completely demolished if you want to build something better in its place.

—I have a cousin who looked gorgeous after the procedure; even her school grades improved.

—It's like buying a diamond that you can show forever. And you, what are you getting done? —asked one of the women. *What a flirt*, I thought, ... *and that straight little nose.*

—No, I'm just keeping her company.

—Your wife? You don't want to leave her alone even for a night?

The staff already knew my relation to Eligia; I couldn't deny it.

—No, my mother.

An air of sisterhood already surrounded them, even though they'd met just a few minutes before. They were all in hospital gowns, smiling, reassuring each other, dreaming of the perfect future they would begin the next day, or at the most in a month, when the edema from the surgery went down; they all had some exaggerated feature that had mortified them their whole lives. Now, perfection was within reach.

The professor didn't perform surgeries impulsively; if he took a case, it was because he found it necessary, as was patently obvious with this group. When I disconnected from the conversation, I thought I had seen a witches' Sabbath. Under the bright light from the window, I imagined what those women would never be again, the versions of themselves that would hide deep in their memories, the features that—unbeknownst to their husbands—they would transmit to their children. I imagined them destroying all the photos from "before," hoping time would help them forget this chapter of their lives. Imperfection was unacceptable. I thought of the Herder School in Montevideo, where students were made to destroy any failed assignments.

The little witches lived the reverse of Eligia's situation: here they were, girls dreaming a future full of promise and within reach; while in the next room a woman dreamt of a known and irrecoverable past.

I left and went to the bar on the street corner.

It was a narrow room, completely different from the watering holes I was used to. Just two small tables that usually remained empty and a short counter that could barely pass for a bar. Only two things contradicted the Lilliputian scale of the place: an oversized espresso machine and a jukebox.

The establishment had exactly four customers when I entered, and they all seemed to be in a hurry to leave and return to their jobs. A young man, probably my age, was serving them: the first and only sober bartender I had met in my life. I stayed drinking for half an hour, until all the other customers left. Then someone interrupted me midthought.

—From the clinic, right? —said a female voice with a strident and imperious tone. The question sounded like an order dictated by someone who has never given orders before, coming from the furthest possible corner of this small establishment. I saw a knee-length skirt, then a loose, crossed blouse with no collar and a single, big button by the hip. The blouse generously revealed parts of her chest, depending on how the baggy flaps fell. What a look for this hour on a workday. Despite the variations of the amount of skin exposed, the minimum was already more than audacious, and constituted the only attractive sight in that unfriendly bar, where I felt forced to rush through my drinks and weigh with each one the possibility of returning to the clinic and not eating lunch. The woman approached me.

—Expensive spot ... Although you, of course ... —She pinched my coat with scorn. —Want to treat me to a drink?

Without asking, the young bartender poured her a chocolate-colored liquid.

—Are you keeping your wife company? Don't tell me you're the one getting plastic surgery.

I did not answer. After a few minutes, I asked for another whiskey, for the road, I said.

—Whiskey? But where are you from ... Ah! South America. Are you a native? ... Do you speak Italian?

—I don't know this city, and I need to find a cheap place to eat. I have enough money to buy you lunch, if you don't ask for anything crazy. But I don't have money for the other thing.

—I know a trattoria just five minutes from here.

We crossed Corso di Porta Vigentina. On the other side of the wall, a pile of rubble hid like a mystery. Then we went into a desolate neighborhood, skirting a large building that was surrounded by a gate with a golden trim. Finally we reached an empty little restaurant where I ordered steak.

—*Paillard? Bisteca?*

—Anything. Meat.

She ordered pasta. I studied the menu, and the prices were very modest. We hardly spoke during the meal. The woman kept looking at me and seemed particularly annoyed every time I poured wine from the jug. When I asked for the check, I almost choked.

—Twelve thousand lire for steak! The menu says three thousand!

—Sir, look again, it says three thousand per *l'etto*.

I looked at the menu. Next to the price of the steak was an asterisk referring to a note on the back of the menu. In a tiny font, it clearly said, *l'etto*.

—What does *l'etto* mean?

—It means a hundred grams —the woman said with a smile.

—My steak was definitely no more than two hundred.

—We always weigh them in the kitchen—replied the waiter calmly, staring at my plate where I had left a few tough tendons that were impossible to cut. —And it was over four hundred grams.

The woman got up to go to the bathroom.

—So —he added— it comes to twelve thousand for the steak, plus salad, wine, pasta, and the soda, for a total of twenty-one thousand.

I paid, and waited in vain for the woman. I was relieved she had escaped, saving me the trouble of cursing her out for her choice of restaurant; the waiter was the only witness to my humiliation. I returned to the bar on Corso di Porta Vigentina and asked the bartender to sell me a bottle of whiskey.

—It's prohibited to sell bottles here . . . Also, if I sell you one, I'll be left with just the bottle that is already open. Why don't you try a liqueur? You can take a bottle for ten thousand.

—Do you have a . . . . ?—"Flask" was another word I hadn't learned from Gassman's films. I made myself understood with a few hand gestures.

—No, this is a serious bar.

I paid for a liqueur with an artificial tangerine color. The woman smiled from the corner. I was trying to fit the bottle in my coat, but the damn thing was impossible to hide: unlike any decent bottle, the body was in the neck, and the base was a cone. She had obviously returned to mock me. I did not smile back.

That night I didn't leave the clinic, and neither Eligia nor I ate dinner.

They came for her at dawn. Everything happened so fast. They unlocked the wheels and slid the bed out of the room. Now it made sense why the doors were so wide; the nurses had to open both door panels to let the bed out. I followed Eligia to the operating room, and waited nearby. As I learned later, the narrow beds outside were only used to remove dead bodies.

It was late in the afternoon when Eligia came out. (A few days later she told me they had given her anesthesia in the room and taken her to the surgery after she was fast asleep. This way she didn't have to see the operating room.) As they came out, several doctors and nurses rushed around her.

—Everything went well—said one of the assistants.

It was only when we were left alone in the room that I was able to really see her: everything was gone. The emergency grafts had been removed, along with the eyelids, revealing the white spheres of her eyes, sunken and motionless. What little remained of the lips was also gone, and the cheek that had suffered the most damage had disappeared, exposing parts of the cheekbone, the jaw, molars, and tongue. Eligia's hair was held inside a cap. I watched her for several hours, unable to look away.

—Everything went well —I said, close to her ear. She moved her head slightly and asked softly for water.

—Everything worked out well —said Professor Calcaterra, later that night. He had come by himself.

He whispered his words in the dark, where I had remained watching Eligia.

—You really think so?

—Yes. I know that her appearance right now is hard to take. It was quite a burn ... not even those from the war ... Allow me to give you some advice. He took me by the arm, and we walked away. —In cases like this, it is necessary to be realistic. As I warned you, this is not about hiding, covering, concealing. It is necessary to accept that a new reality has taken hold. Your father created something new. I can't deny that: so our only option is to let this tragedy run its course, to find a way for it to express itself. We must remove the old ruins, so a new face is free to form, without any of those misleading labyrinths. Life surprises us, you know. Creation can multiply from just a few particles. We had to remove all those ridges, all that excess, and leave only what's essential so the manufacturer can do his work, without detours and distractions. Nothing is better than air and light, if we want these forms to develop in the best way possible. Later on, of course, we will add some grafts. This woman will recover all her functions: her eyelids, her lips, everything. But the aesthetics, that we must leave to nature. Allow the world to familiarize itself with this new form. Only that which is visible can be comprehended; that's what can be altered. But a mystery never changes. How can that improve?

... Don't let it shock you. You must have courage! You didn't truly understand your mother's wounds. Her name is Eligia, correct? Think about this first stage of the treatment as a revelation of light, order, and clarity.

That night I acted as I had in the previous clinic, and didn't change my clothes. I sat on the sofa bed, but after three hours that felt like an eternity, I had slid all the way to the floor. I fell asleep at an angle that suggested my original position. When I woke up, I saw Eligia's face in the glow of the bed sheets, but couldn't comprehend the image. Suddenly, the white surfaces of her face clicked together. Lying in the dark, I stared blankly at the exposed nasal cartilage and its position relative to other white spots on her face. Seen from that angle, her face looked more like a skull that every now and then gasped for air. The missing cheek left a deep hollow. In the dark, colors weren't distinguishable, only degrees of dryness or humidity in a black-and-white image. The perfect teeth that had once only appeared briefly during indecisive smiles were now completely exposed, a curved and elusive series, an immaculate matter, a dispassionate archeology. Meanwhile, in the wide gums, bathed in saliva and pulsating with blood, life simmered.

The following days were consumed by Eligia's care. I barely had time to ask the maids for a sandwich, or run to the bar and ask for a shot of the cheapest liquor they had. I drank all the artificial colors created by chemistry: purples, violets, emerald greens, light and intense yellows. All those bottles the bartender must have kept for decoration, not for serving.

In one of my alcohol runs to the little bar, the woman from the first time greeted me with a smile from her usual corner.

—Hello! You're looking pale. Are you ok?

I didn't answer.

—Still holding a grudge?

I had already become one of the regulars, and one day the bartender welcomed me with a slight smile. When I closed my tab, I realized the price of my drinks had dropped dramatically.

—You are now a regular, so you get the discount —he said. —It was Dina's idea, so you don't go looking for another bar.

On the next visit, encouraged by my new special rate, I decided to have a serious conversation with the bartender about getting rid of those sweet liquors; we had to get some whiskey.

—Too expensive for this bar.

—What about some other dry spirit? Grappa?

—Too pedestrian for my clients. What kind of place do you think I'm running?

The woman came out of her corner and grabbed my hand.

—Come, I'll show you a place where you can buy the stuff you like. And don't give me that pissy face. Don't you know how to trust people?

We walked toward the center of the city, and then into a district that was unknown to me. In one of the shops, my guide asked for a brand of imported whiskey and paid for it.

—Here you go. A peace offering. You don't have a sense of humor, you know. You're a free man, you can throw it away, if you want.

I opened the bottle, took a sip, and put it in my coat. We entered a district with old buildings from the last century that tried to imitate, as economically as possible, the glories of the Renaissance. I don't know which one of us slipped away, but moments later I was walking alone and lost.

* * *

You see, I grew up in a rational city with a grid. On a previous trip here, someone had always guided me, but on this occasion, I was free to follow my own steps, wandering though capricious streets skirting walls that no longer existed, or perhaps workshops that had once produced weapons or silk: not for war or seduction, but to sell to the rest of Europe. These buildings were now gone, leaving behind wider sidewalks or small plazas. No direction was constant, no reference, stable; there was no checkerboard framing the whole. The width of these arteries was indeterminate; sometimes it varied abruptly, sometimes the transitions were imperceptible. The truth is I couldn't tell if I was walking on a street, an avenue, or through a plaza.

This uncertainty took a turn for the worse when a thick fog began to descend over the city; the first great fog of the year. I could barely see ten meters ahead of me. I tried to stay on the sidewalk, sometimes marked only by a yellow line or a thin cord, and never too reassuring for pedestrians. In an unexpected corner, a car nearly ran over me as it cut through the symbolic sidewalk. I didn't feel safe. It seemed to me that I was passing through a succession of disconnected fragments. I asked a man, who was obviously cold and rushing somewhere, how to get to Corso di Porta Vigentina.

—It's far … You need to turn there. He gestured with his elbow in an imprecise direction. —Take Viale Regina Margherita, which changes into Viale Caldara … When you get to Porta Romana … Let's see … Then you would have to turn around … No, no …

The more lost he got in his own explanation, the less suspicious he seemed of me.

—You should really do this: from the plaza, take Corso di Porta Vittoria to Viale Sforza. All the way ... Actually—he said after a brief pause—it might be better if you go to the plaza and ask someone else!

I tried to follow his directions, but failed to find the plaza and got lost again. I saw the façade of a building giving way to a semicircular arch with a huge door. The whole thing seemed to be designed by an architect with the intention of compressing the poor devils that had to go in and out every day. By the door, there was a small recess, a kind of hallway that led to a smaller entrance covered in graffiti.

That's where I sat to drink. To my right there was trash: empty boxes with faded labels, a car bumper, a broken toilet. These old pieces retained their joy, or recovered it only because someone wanted to turn them into trash. Somehow they had escaped the thoroughness of the Milanese municipal services, and I imagined what a nice effect they produced next to the graffiti. I took another sip from my bottle and went back to the street to get a better perspective. Not bad. Not bad at all! The simple drawings complemented what must have been a curse word, next to a pile of metal and cardboard objects.

I looked around. The small recess was hidden, dwarfed, besieged by the gigantic arch that sheltered it and was itself inscribed in a series of equal arcs that faded into the fog. Outside this entryway, all color was insufficient, unnecessary. Between the arches, the cyclopean stones were pressed together, squeezing the interior with a suffocating weight. Light turned these gray stones into a wet coat, shrunken and several sizes too small for the scale of the great volumes. I looked anxiously for a boundary, for right angles that could give me a sense of the building, encompass the whole, frame the tensions, place them in a reliable certainty. But the more I looked, the more these crushing forces seemed to appear in the concavity. This kind of architecture, ominous and gigantic, ended up without any reference points: high above, it was lost in a dull, colorless glow concealing the sky; to the sides, it receded into the darkness of the street. Any continuity, any sequence, any reproduction, was truncated. My little recess in the side of the entryway looked like a slit of color. I returned to it, and when I bent down, the alcohol finally hit my brain. I staggered, I sat, but it wasn't very comfortable. Through the walls I felt the huge blocks pressing down. I drank some more whiskey, tucked my feet in, and wrapped myself with my coat. I was sound asleep when a voice snapped at me: —You can't sleep here. Come on!

A man dressed in municipal overalls tapped me with his mop. He was frightened, and his freckled face showed repugnance. I got up and resumed my aimless walk. —Southerners!—he yelled as he collected the abandoned junk and threw it in his cart.

IV

AS WINTER APPROACHED, MY life in Milan felt even more trapped by the routine. I started sleeping on the sofa bed without changing out of my street clothes. The first few mornings of my new habit, the maid reproached me:

—Why don't you open the bed? What a strange boy you are! If you had been educated before the war, you would not be so lazy. Young men used to make their own beds and always look sharp and clean. What a man that Mussolini! What a shame that he made a mistake with his foreign policy ...

Wasn't I saving her the trouble of having to fold back the sofa bed and push it against the wall? Thanks to me she only had to fold a blanket.

A few days later, she stopped making comments.

Stripped of so much facial muscle, Eligia entered a period of stillness. For me, the biggest inconvenience was the lack of eyelids. I would read to her for an hour or two in the morning and in the afternoon, but I could never tell if she was asleep.

Her pupils could be present and alert, or absent, meaning she was asleep, but mostly they remained in a half state, partially concealed, somewhere between consciousness and sleep. From time to time, she interrupted my reading to tell me the last passage she remembered—usually something a few pages back, so I had to return and start again. It wouldn't have bothered me to repeat entire sections had we been reading a good book, but the first shipment we got from home consisted of trite novels and self-help magazines, the kind that drop priceless wisdom like: "your illness is a wonderful opportunity to start a new life." The only one we enjoyed was a pop sociology book about everyday life, spiced up with a theory about alienation, though it was of the rosy kind. I wrote to my family specifying the types of books Eligia preferred. In November we received a few novels of the Latin American Boom and issues of a history magazine in which some of Aron's stuff had been published. The most recent one included an article with a description of a battle, a sordid, fratricidal struggle, recalled by one of its participants. The manuscript had been found shortly before our departure to Milan.

—

... That cold morning, I woke up our dear commander with some mate before sunrise. Other comrades joined us, and some brought their own gourds. Considering the imminent battle and the bone-chilling cold, the commander allowed them to stay and even kissed some of the vessels as we passed them around. Moments later, he clutched our red-and-black flag and got on his horse, a thin and temperamental foal. He said that trotting the horse helped rally the fighting spirits of his soldiers, but the whole thing seemed like

vanity to me. Unfortunately, he'd had his horseshoes replaced that morning, so the animal began to slip as soon as we entered the muddy grasslands.

Despite the limited visibility, we were able to discern the strange white cross of our enemies, which struck me as heretical. A thick, bluish mist, uncommon in this region, made it impossible to see how many they were. Our heroes and those savages charged toward each other with enthusiasm; but, at the sound of the first shot, both armies turned around and scattered. After a while, officials from both sides managed to regroup their troops, but the men refused to attack again. Our commander, trying to rile up his men, trotted his horse and gave a speech that was surely glorious, but ultimately lost to the wind, as no one was able to record it for historical posterity. Then he drew his weapon and charged. Not a single man followed.

The front lines still remained, but these cowards knew only how to aim their gazes at each other. From that point on, everything I remember is inexplicable and extraordinary. When the commander realized he was riding alone, he tried to halt his horse, but the animal seemed possessed and continued running toward the enemy as everyone stared in disbelief. Finally, the beast slipped on the mud and my commander went flying. I rode as fast as I could to the site of the fall and tried to help him get up, but he was so drunk from all the prebattle brandy, he kept falling. This was our precarious situation when the enemy line began to advance toward us, perhaps out of curiosity at the inexplicable scene they were witnessing. Finally, I grabbed the commander by the collar and shouted:

—You are on your own, you drunken bastard. I'm going back!

At that precise moment, a rock struck the poor man and knocked him out cold. I barely had time to get on my horse when I found myself surrounded by our adversaries. Surely, my time had come, but, incredibly, they simply stood there. I could not believe my eyes. I looked at my commander, thinking he would not be in this humiliating situation if our so-called army weren't such a bunch of cowards.

It was then—and I swear by my honor this was against my will—that I found myself riding along with this cavalry. The armies finally met face-to-face, and what must be the most unusual event in the history of military tactics ensued. When a wing from either side attacked, its counterpart pulled back, and then the opposite wing counterattacked. The result was a continuous rotation around the axis where I was standing. This extraordinary dance lasted several hours and without any casualties. It was almost like a contradance or minuet. Eventually, the commander's troops—he, by the way, was passed out somewhere—began to press on both the opposition's flanks until I was freed from my captivity. I embraced my heroic comrades, and we cheered as the enemy retreated. But then, some idiot accused me, of all people, of having collaborated with the enemy. And so the brutes, who had been hugging me just a few minutes before, began to beat the hell out of me, ignoring my pleas, my tears, and my explanation, which was as follows: The cape I was wearing was a gift from my dear mother to protect me from inclement weather. It was one of the capes she used to sell at her stand in the market; it was the only one left after she had sold the rest to a group of officers from the other side. These capes were in high demand, because my mother made them using the ancient techniques of the Andean peoples. Somehow, she was able to weave them in a way that made them waterproof. That was why I had decided to wear my cape on this rainy day, not realizing that our enemies would assume that I was one of them.

My simple explanation was ignored, and I was about to become the only casualty of the battle, when we suddenly saw a column advancing toward us. I shouted: —The savages are coming back with reinforcements!—and the wimps, who were about to cut my head off, took off running like lost souls. I was left behind, no horse, no weapons, but alive. I waited for our enemy's impending arrival, next to the commander, who was still snoring. But then I realized that the column was actually one of our patrols, which we had sent the night before to scout the enemy's position and we had completely forgotten them. I was arguing with the officer in charge of the patrol, when we saw a few men on horseback approaching in the distance. According to the officer, they had not joined the battle because their orders had been to observe, not to engage in combat. They left, and, for a second time, I was left alone in the open.

As it turns out, the men approaching on horseback didn't belong to either side, but had come to deliver some livestock to the opposing army. They treated me with great consideration and offered me their best horse. I was astonished, but kept my mouth shut because they were carrying enormous knives. Not long after, I arrived with them at the enemy camp. I was about to fall to my knees and start begging for mercy, when one of the men started explaining to the others what he had seen: in essence, I, with no horse or weapon, had fought the entire enemy patrol and forced them to retreat. As soon as he was done, these glorious soldiers appointed me as their new marshal. That night, as we sat around the fires and the grills, everyone discussed the real-life legend of my immeasurable courage. I was now chief of this courageous army. I decided that the next morning we would march toward the savages—who had once entrapped me with their deceptions—and impose on them the principles of real civilization by any means necessary.

The next day we went into the city and rounded up the criminals who had once lied to make me their comrade-in-arms. Seeing the look in their eyes as we cut their heads off was quite the sight! My men left their knives in the juicy heads.

Finally, they brought me the commander, that drunk who made me risk my life and had never even considered elevating my rank, much less, giving me a medal. I made him kneel over raw peas and ordered him to look at the heads of his accomplices, now displayed on stakes.

I made him stay in that position for four days, until all the flies and vultures had scraped the skulls clean. I was going to behead him as well, but the guards pointed out that it was useless: the man had lost his mind and now talked to the skulls as if they were the only beings who could understand him …

Years later, when I was already a senator, I passed that exact spot and saw a silver pea plant covered with bits of paper. A villager told me it had grown from the peas my rival had kneeled on, and that they were very miraculous. Legend was that he had wandered around for years performing miracles, until one day a bolt of lightning took him into the sky.

—

—Mario, I fell asleep.

—During which part?

—When the officer switched sides.

The narrator had switched sides so many times I decided to read the article again from the beginning. I remembered the horrifying conclusion in time, and told Eligia that it wasn't worth reading to the end.

* * *

The pace of the surgeries accelerated, or at least that is how it felt to me. The clinic was so uneventful time seemed to fly.

At Christmas, a priest came to visit, but Eligia had been in surgery just two days prior and couldn't receive him. That was the only time we didn't share the floor with at least five or six big noses, but she was so intent on advancing her treatment, she didn't want to wait until the end of the holidays.

The professor came often and demonstrated both scientific and human interest in her case. When daylight in Milan was already exhibiting that shadowless quality that characterizes winter—that faded gray that pairs so well with gold, red, and blue, but crushes the spirit when it spans everything—the professor studied Eligia's face closely and remarked:

—We're making progress.

He said this while tracing invisible spirals with his index finger. Then he addressed me. —See how the situation has simplified. There are no more labyrinths. We're getting to the root of the problem. Her body is helping: see how the lips of her wounds are conforming to each other. It shows we're working with a being in harmony. Now that we have overcome the chaos, we can heal the lesions that are at least coherent using keloids.

As he walked to the door, he gave me a frank smile and handed me a small piece of paper from his pocket.

—Study Latin. Learn from your mother. What are you going to do all this time, here in Milan, without friends?

I put the paper away, suspecting it was something Eligia wasn't supposed to see. I went to the bathroom and read it:

VITRIOL: *Visita Interiorem Terrae Rectificando Invenies Operas Lapidem.*

Visit the interior of the earth, and by purifying what you find there, you will discover the hidden stone.

If during our reading sessions my throat got too dry, I would wait for Eligia to doze off and go to the bar. Several times I bumped into the woman who had taken me to the trattoria; she would be pacing around or leaning against the wall in Corso di Porta Vigentina. She dressed in a simple style, at least when compared to the dresses her colleagues wore in other districts of the city, places a bit redder than the boring neighborhood of the clinic. I would often find her shivering. The stuff she wore was no good for the cold or the rain.

For better or worse, she was the only person I could talk to, so I took on the habit of treating her to whatever she wanted, usually warm chocolate milk. Her name was Dina Rovato. While we talked, she kept an eye on the corner outside where her clients usually met her. If a car drove up, she would whisper, "Sorry, a client," and run out of the bar. As soon as she was gone, the bartender would take her glass, meaning that when she came back—usually twenty minutes later—I would have to buy her another chocolate milk if I wanted to keep talking.

In one of our first meetings she asked me who the woman at the clinic was.

—Who told you I am with a woman at the clinic? Have you been gossiping with one of the maids?

—No!—Dina said laughing—the maids don't talk to me; they don't even come around here ... who can stand those pretentious women? I was just asking.

—She's very important, one of the most beautiful women from my country. She's paying me to accompany her while she gets plastic surgery.

—It's odd that she wouldn't prefer the company of another woman.

—She needed someone who could protect her. Her enemies are powerful. You don't know how things are back in my country.

—It's odd that you accepted this kind of work ... I don't believe you ... How did you learn Italian?

—From Gassman's films.

Dina hesitated for a few seconds. Finally, she said:

—There's something weird about you, I don't know what. Then she added in a serious tone:—Why don't you tell me?

—Why don't you just drink that disgusting stuff and go fuck yourself.

After that exchange, we didn't talk again for a couple of weeks. I would see her in her usual spot when I went to the bar. From time to time I saw a smile in her eyes, but no sarcastic looks. Then one night, she came into the bar with another man.

—I introduce you to my prince —she said to him. —He's the one who raped me for the first time. Be careful because he's South American. He carries a knife and knows how to protect women.

The man gave me a fearful look. He ordered two *ristrettos.*

—Get him a drink too. —Dina added.

I ordered whiskey before the man could even open his mouth. He looked anxious.

—Touch me, dear. Don't be afraid, this is my little brother, who respects me a lot.

—Of course —said the man, keeping his eyes on me.
Dina also looked at me.
—The gentleman here wants to invite us to his apartment.
I shrugged.

We had only driven a few blocks, and I already felt lost in that city of eccentric circles. We arrived at a small, damp apartment. There was no whiskey, no wine, nothing. I complained. The man came up to me, now with a look of contempt and ridicule; he was some fifteen centimeters taller than me. He threw some bills on the table and said: —Go buy whatever you like, there's a shop right across the street; but your passport stays. I want you back.

—The passport goes where I go. I leave my coat and that's enough.

Two hours later the gentleman and I were both completely drunk. Dina kept whispering things into the man's ear as they lay on the sofa. I stayed at the other end of the room. A dramatic, operatic voice played from a record.

Suddenly, Dina's voice overlapped with the music. It was her usual tone of insecure arrogance, but this time it also sounded almost bureaucratic.

—Come Mario, be a good boy and rape me.

I took my pants off in a mechanical motion and expressed just how boring I found the whole thing. Dina, who was still wearing her skirt, tried to compensate for my reluctance by exaggerating a theatrical resistance. Her pubic hairs moved like ant legs going nowhere. The man looked attentively and, aroused, ordered:

—Hit her.

—I won't hit anyone.

—It's better if you do it —said Dina in a low voice.

—What, are you afraid of a whore? —the man insisted.

—If you like this, good; if you don't, then good night. I won't hit anyone.

—Let me see; stand back a little, but don't pull out.

Dina's body, still dressed, fluttered in the dark as she feigned pleasure. I was barely moving. The man began to spank her calmly, but with all his might. I felt Dina cringing in pain, but still pretending to be raped. My hands, which held Dina's arms, received two distinct messages of pain: one, continuous, from her disembodied movements pretending to resist rape; another, spasmodic, authentic, that ran through Dina like electricity when the man hit her. She tried not to scream and buried her head on the couch, but her breathing skipped when he struck her. The man knew how to produce suffering without leaving a mark, he was no novice; he knew where to hit with his hand closed and where to hit with his palm. When, after a punch, Dina moaned involuntarily, the punishment ceased. The man ordered her:

—Now suck him, but make him come outside your mouth.

Dina applied herself obediently and was busy for a long time, until the man, disappointed, exclaimed:

—So?

Neither one of us answered. Finally, he pushed Dina away from me, glanced resentfully at my erect penis and said:

—Ask me to cut it.

—Listen—I said. —I have a knife in my coat.

—Bravo! I'll give you money. I'll give you all the money you want, little South American. It will be an economic miracle! A small superficial cut at the base, as if I were castrating you, just enough to see a little blood, since you have no milk. You know I don't want any trouble. I'm a good person. It's just an innocent whim.

I went and got the knife the stewardess had given me and flicked it open with the blade toward him.

—I've got this knife because I'm going to cut you open if you keep babbling about castrating me.

—C'mon, just a tiny cut, you'll hardly even see it, I've done it a lot before. What is it to you? You're outside your country. What do you care? These whores? If you give me this small pleasure, you'll earn some money.

I pushed the blade against his face and he looked me in the eyes.

—What did you think ... that I was being serious?! They warned me you South Americans could be dangerous. You don't know how to play, you're all bad down there.

He opened his fly and put his penis in Dina's mouth. A few seconds later he said excitedly:

—Keep sucking and don't take it out!

Dina made some muffled sounds as the man ejaculated, then he pulled out and exclaimed: —Don't, don't spit it out, but don't swallow it either. Now go and spit it on your South American's hair. I'll give you an extra five thousand lira.

Dina hugged me tenderly and rubbed her cheek against mine. Then she started kissing my head and with every kiss she let out some of the warm contents of her mouth. Once done, she lit a cigarette. While the man was washing, she whispered in my ear: "Sorry, but I need the money ... you're good;

I don't like putting you through this. Now you're my friend, I mean it. Why didn't you come? After so many months here? Do you have some little nurse in that clinic?"

Still trapped in a permanent erection, I'd felt paralyzed after feeling the moisture on my scalp, but suddenly there was also an intense awareness of my body as I sat on that carpet and leaned against the sofa. I became acutely aware of Dina's wet vulva and the man's damp member. I thought of men and their ridiculous cocks, women and their ridiculous wet vulvas, both hidden in underwear, while their owners went shopping, greeting each other with so much ceremony, buying and selling stupidities. I felt a drop run down my back and I burst into laughter. The man looked at Dina and made a motion with his index finger:

—Pour him a drink.

I could barely contain my laughter, which stopped for brief intervals, but three drinks later I was still overcome with laughing fits.

When I returned to the clinic, I didn't have the energy to shower. The next morning my hair was matted with dry semen and gel. My pillow was also a mess, but I didn't take any precautions, and the maid didn't seem to notice the stains.

Eligia was going through the most brutal period of her treatment: the bones of her jaw and her nose cartilage were visible. The sections exposed to the air had yellowed and those underneath, thin organic membranes, almost like cuticles, remained white. That day, she asked me to read her an article, the last one for a few days, since the next morning she was scheduled for another surgery.

* * *

The following day, she came out of the operating room with a large cast around her chest and an orthopedic brace with straps and buckles that immobilized her left arm at a right angle above her head. Her forearm was resting on her crown. A strip of flesh extended from the arm to the lower part of her chin. The doctors called it a "flap," but this one was tense and allowed no movement.

In the following days, Eligia developed her own sense of kinetics. At the first clinic, she had identified certain movements that allowed her to study the changes in her body without using mirrors or her hands. She used gestures and quivering movements, similar to what horses do to ward off flies. In Milan, after this particular surgery, she developed a gymnastics around the flap. Any body movement was articulated in relation to this tensed strip of skin. Compared with the original plan of our human anatomy, her possibilities for movement were few, and it became even harder for her to do anything on her own. The doctors explained that this was a crucial stage of the treatment; thanks to the flap they had something to work with. Eligia took pathetic precautions to ensure their success. Through the hole in her cheek, I could see her teeth clench tightly whenever she had to change positions even slightly.

Two nights later I bumped into another group of formerly big-nosed young women in the corridor, who had been operated on by Calcaterra's assistants in between serious procedures.

Some started chatting with me about the usual stuff: "How is it down there? How is it for Italians? Are you a native?" It was a strange kind of flirtation coming from women who, twenty-four hours before, were convinced they were ugly, and now thought they were beautiful, despite the massive swelling, the purple cauliflower ears, and the bandages that covered their noses and forced them to speak short phrases in nasal tones, quickly running out of breath. The truth is no one really knew what they would look like when the bandages came off.

The one who seemed most interested in chatting was a brunette with short hair in a light-blue gown, who liked to throw some English words into the mix of open Italian vowels, the cutting, labiodental sounds of the Milanese dialect, and a forced French nasality produced by the bandages. It was hard to understand what she was saying, but I was entertained by all these heterogeneous sounds coming from her mouth and I liked how her body looked in the two-dimensional gown, which had complicated patterns and was fastened at the neck with a large button.

The nurses addressed her with particular deference and tried to anticipate all her wishes, which made me think she was the daughter of one of the owners of the clinic or a member of some influential family. She was very young and said to me: —You know, I have a cousin over there. He left at the end of the war, as soon as they lifted the restrictions on emigrants. His name is Peter Schweppes. Do you know him?

—No, there are a lot of people there. Why did he leave?

—Silly things … political stuff.

One by one, the other patients went back to their rooms and we were left alone. The shift nurse smiled at us and said: —Time to go to sleep, it is late …

—I don't know why, but I don't feel sleepy—the girl said.

We talked until late. Her name was "Sandie" Mellein; she was still in high school and lived with her father in Milan. She shared fairly personal matters with me, but, in those years, it wasn't unusual for strangers to discuss their lives in a first meeting, due to the popularity of Freud. Those conversations didn't reveal anything important about the person, but served to break the ice and start a more intimate relationship. After a few hours, her secrets began to get repetitive, and we realized we were running out of things to talk about.

—Is Sandie short for Sandra or Sarah?—I asked, but she just shrugged her shoulders without answering. Sandie had an impulsive way of talking. The bandages, plus the swelling around her eyes, made it difficult to discern her features. She had the habit of moving her left hand as she talked, as if to emphasize her point, except the motions were completely divorced from her words.

She was telling me banalities about her schoolmates and her family. I noticed she used English words like *beach boys* when talking about her trips to Hawaii, or *cereal* (which she pronounced "Syria," the final *el* sound barely peeping out of her throat as if in a pedantic hypercorrection) when she ordered breakfast the following morning. Without my asking, she shared her age—seventeen—and asked mine.

—Ah! Twenty-three. You're a full-grown man.

—A six-year difference in age isn't that much—I said. My father Aron was twenty years older than my mother.

I was trying to follow Sandie's banal words, when, subconsciously, I blurted out: —That's how they ended.

I felt the urge to leave and go to Eligia's room or the bar, but to get my mind off this temptation, I focused all my attention on my interlocutor. Her family was from Milan. They owned the factory that manufactured the popular Cavaliere Marco stockings, and had recently started producing textiles as well. I asked her why they didn't use a more feminine-sounding name for the product, something like "Soft Skin" or "Peach." As it turns out, the name of the founder, her great-great-grandfather, was "Marco," and so the stockings would be called Marco forever.

Sandie wore a short puffed hairstyle with bangs, a courageous feat, considering that just a day earlier she had been under general anesthesia while some unknown surgeon hammered her nose to pieces.

I tried to remember if I had seen her before the operation. Either I hadn't, or she hadn't made any impression on me. That's how I missed my only chance to see the original Sandie. It was obvious she couldn't wait to flirt with her new face, and a foreigner was the perfect subject for such an experiment. She wanted to experience the first love of her new beautiful life, the romance that would mark a break from previous years, the era of her long nose. I had been chosen as the testing ground for her seductions, a witness that would have to disappear after her grimaces had been perfected.

—I have a soul that is kind of diffuse, as if a parchment screen separated the conscious and subconscious parts of my mind. The conscious part is nocturnal, lunar, as the *Bella* horoscope says ... This is confirmed by an American psychologist who used Freud's theories to establish scientific categories of the female mind in a book called *The Goddess You Will Be*. Due to my mother's absence at an early age and the kind of relationship I have with my father, it is very clear that I am governed by the goddesses that symbolize personal liberation, such as Athena or Shiva. Now that I'm going to be beautiful, I must prevail over my tendency to explore my "preconscious" and act according to the orders of *the id.* I have to learn to look into the mirror without fear. For an Aries like me, this is the perfect time for big changes, and that's why I decided to get the surgery now. Did you know that for Freud, anatomy is destiny? That's why the most direct way to affect my fate is with this surgery. There's a psychic, here in Milan, who specializes in the combination of astrology and Freud's theories. I consulted with her several times before the surgery, of course, and she told me that, thanks to the conjunction of Jupiter and Saturn, my cosmic urges would be able to shape me from the inside, supported by the external modeling of Professor Calcaterra. Now that the ascendancy of Jupiter influences my nose, it is the best period to transform my old personality ... *This is the right way.*

And she went on.

—When I've recovered, you can come visit my house —she said suddenly, and with confidence, as if she already had control of her first admirer.

The next morning, Eligia, still swollen from her last surgery, asked me to read her another article from one of the magazines that had come with the last shipment.

We present this piece, which is the result of one of the most detailed journalistic investigations ever carried out in South America. Thanks to an enormous effort, and after almost one year of tracking this complicated trail, we can present what must be considered the definitive truth about one of the most jealously guarded mysteries of our time: the fate of the embalmed body of the General's wife, who dominated the history of the twentieth century in these latitudes. We are proud to have succeeded where the best correspondents failed. The material presented in this article is supported by signed declarations and videotapes stored in secure facilities...

With her usual energy, the General's wife fought against her perennial enemies, the rich. When asked to see a doctor about her ever more frequent bleeding, she answered: "Never! Doctors are a bunch of oligarchs. They want to eliminate me!" While she refused to get medical help, an eminent foreign scientist was shocked to receive a proposal from a secret government emissary.

—But how could I possibly go along with something like this! The woman is alive. This is sacrilege!

The great scientist wasn't an oncologist or a clinical doctor; his area of specialty was embalming, and after a career of studies and experiments, he had developed an astonishing method for corpse preservation.

As it became clear that the matter had been decided and the proposed fee was increased, the genius started to give in, and, half an hour after her death, he got to work, preparing for his complex techniques, which included massive tubs with cranes and other devices that were usually reserved for moving patients with multiple fractures or severe burns.

The professor's method had been perfected to such degree that it was possible to complete this "treatment for eternity" without touching the body. The scientist ordered absolute secrecy regarding the work taking place in the rooms of the Presidential Palace. There was good reason for so much secrecy. The body had to be completely dehydrated and stuffed before it could be returned to its original beauty.

No one betrayed the secret, except an errand boy who was barely an adolescent. He said he caught a glimpse through a door that opened briefly. Turning pale, he described a terrible sight: a wrinkled mummy with petrified skin, like purple ore, and ridges surrounding dark abysses of dead and evaporated flesh. All of this remained in the imagination of a young man who opened his mouth and disappeared forever. Was he forced to spend the rest of his life in an insane asylum, as some claim? Did the custodians take matters into their own hands? Was it a case of simple modesty? All speculation is useless. This period will remain a secret forever. What is evident is the beauty of the final result, though for the nearly two years it took to complete the treatment, not even the General dared to look at his wife. Only once did he see the body from afar, submerged in pungent chemicals, and the military man turned white to the point that his bodyguards thought he was having a heart attack.

Finally, from the rooms that some of the staff had come to call the "Clinic of Eternity," emerged not the President's wife, but an angelic doll: it was her, no doubt, but when she was twelve; her beauty was more perfect, her skin even whiter and more impeccable, and her soul still free from the suffering brought on by politics and disease. For his part, the great sage told the press: —It is a perfect job. This body will never decay. Only fire or acid could destroy it.

—Did they include photos of the embalmed body? —asked Eligia.

—No, only when she was alive —I said.

Eligia wasn't interested in those. The article went on to describe the incredible series of adventures this woman's body endured after the General was deposed, and its eventual disappearance. All the clues proved to be false, even the ones that led to Europe.

Eligia seemed particularly interested in the part where the next civil president—he'd appointed Eligia as head of primary education and was the leader of her political party (one of reasonable, educated people, who seemed to be the exact opposite of the fiery partisans surrounding the General)—declared that the body had been destroyed with acid. According to some rumors, Eligia had an affair with this politician, and this is what unleashed Aron's fury.

The article chronicled even more unbelievable adventures. It concluded with a secret report, allegedly drafted by one of the military officials who planned the disappearance of the body. The final paragraphs set the action aboard a ship:

After a few minutes, the priest emerged from the stairway leading to the cabin. The coffin had been placed on top of an improvised sliding board and was leaning against the railing. There was a tense silence when the priest began the ceremony. The funeral oration rose mournfully above the deck. The cadence of the ritual words was starting to put the men to sleep; they lowered their heads and listened to the final amen.

Then, reduced to its sheer physicality, the coffin tipped overboard, hit the water with a splash, and floated for a few moments before sinking slowly.

The sailors couldn't help but stare at the spiraling movement, so simple, so final; the sounding line indicated the water was twenty-five meters deep ...

I interrupted the reading to clear an old doubt.

—That time as a kid that I was taken to the women's prison with you, was it her order?

—I don't know.

—But you organized an homage to the wife of the Liberator, the same day the others organized a march in her honor.

—Yes, but ours was attended by forty people; theirs had two hundred thousand.

—Anyhow, you hated each other.

She thought long before answering. —Yes—she said.

After I finished reading, we heard a soft knock on the door. It was Sandie, who had finished her "syria-l." I let her in and introduced them to each other with curiosity.

—How are you, Madam? The nurses told me so much about you.

I had been hesitant to invite people to Eligia's room, not knowing whether she would enjoy new company. She had asked me to remember that she could not just get up and leave if something bothered her. I had the feeling that a visit from someone outside the clinic would be unpleasant.

Eligia stared at Sandie's swollen face and said a few friendly words. Sandie took that as a sign that her presence was welcome and started babbling sympathetically, using her Anglicisms and hand gestures. She didn't stay long, ending with:

—After tomorrow, when Mars comes under the influence of Venus, will be a good time to work on the cathexis of your "secondary narcissism." I'm sure your condition will improve a lot!

Before leaving, she insisted that I call her. She gave me her phone number and whispered—... if you don't call me, I'll call you.

Then she approached Eligia with her cheek out and lips pursed to give her one of those women kisses—cheek to cheek. Fortunately, she realized what a gaffe this was, and stopped herself with a smile. The skin on Sandie's arms was olive. It seemed to be made of an impenetrable substance that could perhaps be melted though never penetrated. She had several freckles on her neck, and I wondered why she didn't have them operated as well, until I realized that, considering that she did not hide them, she probably thought they made her look interesting. As for her face, it was still a mystery to me, *it would be a blind date*, as Sandie said.

There was no sound coming from the grand bed after she left, but a few minutes later a murmur rose from the sheets.

—She seems like a proper young lady. You should accept her invitation.

V

AMONG THE FEW VISITS we received in February, one was from the chaplain of the clinic, who seemed very surprised to see Eligia. Serious patients intimidated him. He was a man of regular, classic features, tanned skin, and a network of deep wrinkles fanning out from the corners of his eyes. His thick beard seemed to grow in all directions, white at the temples, gray on the chin, and black above his mouth. His hair, still dark, spilled freely over his ears. His body revealed its humble origins, signs that he had worked for many years out in the open; he was a strange presence in this clinic frequented by rich big-noses. He asked Eligia if she wanted to have confession, and I left before I could hear her answer.

Outside the room, the priest seemed more hesitant than ever. His eyes were open with astonishment, but then he closed them tightly and sank his bearded jaw into his chest. His whole body concentrated on that gesture. Now his wrinkles reconfigured and fanned out of the temples instead. He had made this gesture a few times when I was in the room with him and Eligia. He gave me this astonished look, and said he hoped to see us in the chapel as soon as Eligia could walk. I was welcome to come on my own before she recovered, he said.

As a boy, I had gone through the usual stages of catechism: communion in a dark blue suit with a white bow on my sleeve, and mass on Sundays with a girlfriend so we could chat after the service. Eventually, I stopped complying with the precepts, but I never reached the point of mocking the Catholic symbols. I used to tell my schoolmates that it was foolish to miss out on all the sacred art owned by the church. Also, I liked to emphasize, being Catholic was the only way I knew how to enjoy my sins while drinking, though in moments of great anguish and fear, I would most certainly go into a church and pray for salvation.

In Eligia, I had noticed a soft respect for religion, combined with a weariness that could be the product of having an atheist father or the fact that she had filed for divorce only seven months after marrying Aron. When he attacked her, twenty-eight years later, he had purportedly summoned her to resolve, once and for all, their separation that always ended up in reconciliation—their passionate and ongoing divorce. The legal papers could be interpreted as an inverted treatise on love, not because of what they said—both Eligia and Aron referred to the reasons for the separation in very general terms—but because of the omissions. Every document would begin with: "The divorce agreement is hereby ... " but might as well have concluded with the same words, referring to that quiet, inexplicable zone, where the litigants reconciled, planting the seeds for their next divorce attempt.

Aron, for his part, saw himself as God's rival, or enemy of any deity for that matter, apostrophizing often in his usual long rants. Forget "God be damned!" or simple imprecations of two or three words; he performed entire speeches, as an equal speaking to an equal, writing long letters to God or the Pope that ended up in his moralizing pornographic novels. He had the special ability to always be on the margins of society, but not as most accursed writers, who, behind their critical language, still knock respectfully on the right doors in order to access fame and power. Aron had an absolute sense of the fringe, as if it were his natural habitat, as if he were the creator of the margin itself. In his correspondence with God, he was more accusatory than angry. He assumed His undeniable kindness, and thus His obligation to show it to this Earth, particularly among the wretched. Thus, Aron unwittingly represented a role that he would have never accepted explicitly: that of the complainer, who pointed out the evils of the universe in a tone that, despite its superficial intensity, was really no more than a "Look Miss! Look at what he is doing!"—just like a good old teacher's pet in school. Since God showed no signs of heeding any attention to his speeches and letters, he felt profoundly disappointed. Without a doubt, a key goal of his suicide was to humiliate God. And so, his last act on earth was meant as proof of the extent to which the all-powerful had failed him.

I went to the bar in the evenings, knowing Dina would appear sooner or later. She now treated me with a jovial and familial tone, and we started to talk more, though there was always the possibility that someone would call out to her from a car.

Sometimes her absences were quite brief, and we were able to resume our conversation exactly where we left off: talking about some new product or making fun of her clients or some customer at the bar. But after a while we ran out of things to discuss and realized that we also liked to share a comforting silence, that allowed each person to focus on his or her problems, knowing that the other was there to listen if necessary. After the bar closed at midnight, we sat outside, and if one of her clients was into that kind of thing, I would hop along. If the client made an ugly face, I stayed behind in Corso di Porta Vigentina, drinking from a flask in the still treacherous winter.

One night, Dina entered the bar with a scrawny old man. His flesh was pale and it hung trembling under his chin; perhaps he had Parkinson's or it was just simple excitement. He invited me to accompany him, along with Dina, to his apartment.

—Don't get me wrong. It's for something serious, artistic.

Dina dragged him to a corner and they talked quietly. She showed him five fingers and a few seconds later, four. The old man nodded with resignation, and Dina came back, asking me to accept the invitation and come along.

Our friend lived in a pair of dark, squalid rooms, and we chatted for a few minutes, as if partaking in a not-so-intimate family reunion. After a short silence, the old man looked at Dina and asked—Shall we begin? She nodded with a serious air of authority.

The decrepit owner of the apartment retired to the next room and returned wearing a tutu. His legs and arms were covered by the stretchy fabric, and only his white face was exposed. He was very thin, despite his great, trembling double chin. The old man went to the darkest corner of the room.

The room was illuminated by a single lightbulb, without a shade or cover, and he leaned his forehead against the wall.

—Let's see it —said Dina—show us how brave you are.

With his back to us, he shook his head in silence. Dina insisted several times, assuring him that she was very interested in seeing his art. She spoke in an encouraging way—it was obvious that she had succeeded with him on previous occasions—but the old man, or at least his back, showed a stubborn refusal. Finally, Dina pleaded—Think of this gentleman, who has come all the way from South America just to admire you! How can you disappoint him like this? The old man turned around timidly and mumbled—Well, I guess I'll do it, but only because the critic has traveled from so far away.

There was no device in the room that could produce any music, but that did not stop the old man, who started off with a few *prima ballerina* steps toward the center light. Then he said: —First position, with his feet in a single line and his elbows slightly outward. He performed a basic demonstration of ballet, announcing each step in a low but enthusiastic voice. His steps were clumsy, as if he had learned a little ballet in his childhood and then spent the rest of his life performing tasks that had nothing to do with his body. He repeated each position several times, greeting me with reverence as I applauded with sarcastic enthusiasm. When practicing an *attitude croisée*, he ended up knocking down the only decoration in the room, a sad vase on a table.

The room didn't even have a picture frame, though one could see the nails and dust marks on the gray walls.

Looking desolate, he finally sat on the sofa.

—I've had such a horrible day. First there was the little box that didn't close. Then the bossy customer who made me lose my focus. And of course, my art is so easily affected. I lose my precision.

Dina kneeled next to him on the couch.

—But you were splendid. It was a very beautiful performance.

—You think?

—I am certain. Isn't that right, Mario? Wasn't he perfect? Just as good as the girls from the San Remo ballet.

She nodded me over.

—Oh yes; very much—I added, following her orders—although I noticed a bit of hesitation in the fifth position.

—In the fifth? Is that true, Dina?—he demanded uneasily. Do you think I've regressed so much that I'll have to settle for that company that performs at the Festival?

—Of course not! He's joking. You were always perfect. Besides, what is wrong with the Festival? Everyone sees it.

She stroked the man in a strange way, rubbing his stomach in a circular motion.

—Mario, show him how much you love him.

Dina grabbed my hand and put it on his stomach so I could continue the same weird caress, while she started pulling his nose softly with absurd little movements.

More than an intimate ritual, I interpreted the whole thing as a game, so I decided to outdo Dina with even more nonsensical caresses, except that mine immediately took on a mocking and aggressive undertone. She spent a few minutes patting the top of his head, occasionally stopping to stare at him very closely, before he mumbled—Please, continue.

Among other wonders of tenderness, I invented a special pinch of the calf, while saying to him:

—This is important, it is very good for the muscles and will improve your fifth position.

—Yes, it is very important for my fifth.

But what started as a game on my part slowly became more violent. I knew the old man wouldn't protest or make a scene while wearing his tutu. I started working on his double chin, pulling, shaking, massaging, squeezing, you name it. This game prevented him from making any gestures, since I pulled the skin in the opposite direction of whatever expression he was about to form. The pressure from my hands made any reflection of feeling, be it joy or protest, impossible. Anticipating the reactions of my victim, I ridiculed them before they could appear in his own face. The more helpless he seemed, the more energetically I worked his flaccid flesh.

On the opposite extreme was Dina, who kept patting and kissing: half parody, half affection. Oddly enough, our work areas never overlapped. If I was pulling the man's ear and blowing on it so hard I was almost shrieking, Dina was caressing the opposite shoulder and applying small massages with a single finger.

A month after leaving the clinic, Sandie returned with a box of chocolates for Eligia. She invited me to eat at her house. They had taken off the bandages and the swollenness around her eyes was subsiding. There was something sensual about her attenuated edema—sore, fleshy—and, in a few days, gone forever, since it was highly unlikely that her future husband would hit her. Perhaps a car accident, a tough windshield, and

Sandie would be sexy again, like this second time she visited.

—Go, Mario. It will be good for you —encouraged Eligia.

I accepted without much thought. It was ten days till the date of the invitation. I didn't measure time with usual astronomical measures, but with the services I provided Eligia: breakfast, washing, reading.

Ten days passed, and Sandie phoned to remind me of the dinner that night. The taxi took me to the door of a luxurious building in Corso Magenta, in the northern part of the city. I entered a salon decorated with large tiles, white marble columns, purple satin curtains, and false Empire furniture.

Sandie leaned back on a chaise longue with golden eagles that seemed about to cackle; a roll cushion, upholstered in black like the rest of the piece, provided support. Her edema was almost imperceptible, but it still gave her a slightly wild air. She had calculated the date of the dinner with enough time for her face to recover, although some of the green and purple shadows around her eyes and the interior of her ears still remained.

—How do I look?

—Beautiful.

—But not my best yet. I still need a massage treatment to activate certain muscles and I have to use a corrective mask at night for the next two months. But what really needs work is my internal adaptation. My therapist compares it to childbirth. It's that hard. I have to allow my new face to reflect all the essential features of my personality that were hidden in my previous life. I'll need the help of all the planets and the wisdom of more psychoanalysts.

She raised her arm and placed it next to her head in an odalisque pose. Her father came in, and after the usual greetings and small talk, we moved to the dining room, which was furnished in a completely different style. The fake luxury of the previous room gave way to Renaissance-style furniture, including an oak table supported by massive chimeras. There were no carpets, and the walls were lined with still lifes, also from the Renaissance, which displayed delicacies or hunted animals ready for the pan. It was evident that a more solid, reasonable sensibility had designed the dining area.

My place at the table faced an image from the sixteenth century that I could never have imagined on my own. The frame had a metal plaque that read "The Jurist." Under a cloak with a fur collar was an embellished vest with embroidered flowers and a thick golden chain—a sign that the subject of the portrait was on the emperor's good side—but the coin on the chain didn't have an inscription or any figure. Underneath the waistcoat, where one would expect to see the body of the subject covered by a shirt, three thick volumes were visible, one over the other, dry and soporific, I imagine. The ruff was made of paper sheets, and a black cap covered the head.

All these elements, represented very naturally, framed the strangest face I have ever seen in my life. It was composed of plucked chickens arranged in such a way that a wing formed the eyebrows' ridge, a thigh made up the cheek, and a small chick passed for a massive nose. A fish also appeared folded onto itself, so that its mouth was also the mouth of the subject, while its tail simulated a beard.

The head of the chick was positioned so its open eye was also that of the jurist. When I paid attention to that detail, I was struck by the realization that the little plucked chicken was still alive. The nature of this gaze was something I had never seen: at first sight, it captured the astonishment of the victim, but then it acquired a different gleam, revealing the sinister mind of the strategist. Never, in my sustained interest in art, had I seen a "psychic anamorphosis" so striking—where the brushstrokes simultaneously represented such a naked innocence and a cold and ruthless calculation. It wasn't necessary for the viewer to change his angle to perceive the difference; the trick was in the mind. Whoever scrutinized this portrait had to force himself to see the two aspects of this same painted eye. I was surprised that this face, imagined four hundred years ago, still had the power to reveal two contrary and overlapping states of moral being. Gazing a second time at the portrait, I recognized an element of the painting so focused on evil that it had lost consciousness of itself. It was the same quality I had attributed to rocks, a perversity beyond human possibility, an instrument of transreason suddenly incarnate here in a flesh without feathers, a terrifying and hidden reference to the desert.

—

—I see you like my Arcimboldi ... My dealer says that it is now worth a fortune. Did you know Arcimboldi was from Milan? You can see some of his stained-glass work at the Duomo. I have my guests sit precisely where you are, because everyone sees different qualities in that painting. I'm amused by people's reactions. Some ask me to please take the painting away ... You tell me there are two states of mind overlapping in the eye that never coincide, that you feel as if the viewer were being forced to swallow a contradiction

he doesn't want to carry within and that will probably spoil his appetite. Interesting... I see very clearly a lack of will. Think about this. What provokes one's fascination if not the evident contrast between the clothes and books of the jurist, which represent social order, and the facial chaos? That contrast obviates what is absent from the portrait. Do you know what is missing from the plucked flesh replaced by meats that aren't its species, like the fish? Will! The will to act, to dominate, to cohere... Did you know that Arcimboldi studied the writings of Leonardo? And do you know what he did with them? He cleaned his pants off with them!

Well, my friends and I share that attitude! Don't come to us with your Florentine idealism. We are people of action and work, even in art. You, who show so much sensibility, have a lot to learn about this city. It isn't this modest merchant who can teach you, but someday I'll introduce you to my friend the art dealer; he's the one that explained to me the significance of this painting and its value. I inherited it along with the furniture in this room from Sandie's mother, but my late wife had her head full of traditionalist prejudices. Don't tell me this Arcimboldi didn't see things with a degenerate audacity. I hate him so much it fascinates me. No perspective, no rational space, no localized movement! According to my art dealer, Arcimboldi discovered that juxtaposition, the lack of perspective, and scale bare the flesh more effectively than any rational reflection. With perspective, there's only a copy of nature; the lack of scale, the combination of meats, express irrationality in each being, and thus, the absence of rules.

Flesh that is subject to the fork or the cannon.

Arcimboldi turned the encyclopedia into a labyrinth; Linnaeus into a stew; anatomy into something that one eats; and all of this into a substance that precedes the encyclopedia, Linnaeus and anatomy! Our Milanese artist didn't choose just any topic. He chose organic matter, the edible, and he is even more famous for the faces he composed with ripe fruits and large vegetables.

—Yes, yes … I've seen some of those in Vienna and in my country.

—How can there be fruit works by Arcimboldi in your country? There isn't enough culture down there. Besides, they cost a fortune ever since surrealism became a thing. Not to mention the Arcimboldi works that my art dealer calls "carnal," the ones with compositions of pigs, fish, game, and birds. I wonder if he built real models before painting. Can you imagine his servants waiting for the master to be done so they could binge on the model? A face of roast chickens on a body of books. Gastronomic anthropology! Intestinal wisdom! A head with edible matter for teeth, and a body that can be consumed with the eye. Can you imagine anything more sensual than the face as the stomach's object of desire? And to top it off, the stomach of the observer as well! The figure, the thought, and the action are all gathered in the same act … That is Milan, a place where power is always authentic, where the political factions started with all their willpower. Then they went to Rome … and Rome … well, you know … Milan doesn't want to be Rome. They have always been the kingdom of heat and bureaucracy. Files over work. No, Milan doesn't want to be Rome. We don't need those waves of tourists during the summer. Milan is always herself, the only Italian city that remains Italian year-round … Milan could have been Venice, did you know that? I still remember the navigli, the network of canals with a port in Porta Ticinese. I remember them so well: the stone bridges and stairways descending into the water. There wasn't as much gold and ostentation as in Venice, but, had we wanted, a little "architectural sanitation"

would have been enough, and there you have it: a second Venice! But no. We decided to cover the canals, bury Venice ... Yes, it is true, we didn't need those disrespectful tourists. We, the Milanese, made the Italian miracle with our own hands. And besides, there is no lack of miracles here; what is lacking now is order and a fighting spirit, someone that can create that order! Yes, Milan is a fighter. You must think that before, with fascism, this was a different city. Isn't that what you think? Tell me!

—No! I agree with everything you say!

—Democracy doesn't bother me, so long as we can do business, but I recognize that the Mussolini of earlier times was a hell of man. You should have seen how he liquidated the general strike Turati organized in '31. He made mistakes later on with foreign policy. But his domestic program! Law and order, and all the trains ran on time. In Italy, getting trains to run on schedule is a true revolution, right up there with the French or Industrial! Milan already had in place the fascism of work, of order ... The alternative was those partisan communists, who only wanted to intimidate women and entrepreneurs. I remember December of 1944 when they blew a bomb in a movie theater.

—Horrible! I consider myself a personal enemy of violence, you know.

—But Mussolini came and traveled all over Milan, standing on a convertible car. Everybody was clapping in the streets. He represented peace! He went to the Teatro Lirico and rallied the people against the communists. What a speech!... Poor man, deep inside, he sacrificed for us. When the Nazis rescued him from Campo Imperatore, he didn't want anything to do with politics, but Hitler forced him to take over Salò, that Social Republic that was nothing. "If you don't"—he said to the Duce—"we will treat

Italy like Poland." Mussolini really understood Italy. Look at those residential laws: everyone in their house, their town, their region! Isn't that fair? Tell me!

—Fair enough. There is no better place than home.

—Now, instead, they send us all these southerners ... The purpose of the Italo-Abyssinian War was to have a place to send our emigrants and not lose them, like all the ones who ended up in South America and were lost forever. What an absurd situation! Italians of pure stock working in a British semicolony ... Back in the thirties, my schoolbooks already had illustrations of the plains in your country with English trains: a semicolony, and our people there, exposed to who knows what vices— effeminacy—in that county of milk and honey ... Racial laws? Here? Well ... some were promulgated, to appease Hitler, but when the ministers asked him, the Duce would reply, "Ignore them!" Only once, in all those years of war, when traveling for business through Dalmatia, did I come across a group of civilians guarded by officers. I asked the soldiers what these people had done, and they replied: "They're Hebrews; we're taking them north." Only once in all those years and it wasn't even in Italy. Also, all those civilians being taken north were very well dressed and carried regal suitcases. Don't believe what you see in movies today. You ask me about the gypsies? But what do you think? That this is Seville?... It is also not true that those years of war saw incredible scarcity. Perhaps a little, but you could go to Florence, in Via Manzoni, or to Biffi Boutique, and order the best risotto and some wine, all for one lira, and they gave you mandarins on top of that. And what risotto! None of those sauces the French like to eat without even knowing what's in them. Here we like everything to be clear: a bit of broth, tomatoes, parmesan, mozzarella, and oregano, all well separated and served

directly on the rice. Every ingredient in plain sight—not like now when they charge you a fortune for pretentious dishes made with leftovers. I remember that even during the worst times of the war, we were kicking glass from the dome of the Boutique and we still had everything we needed. What a sight this city was! The Hotel del Corso left in ruins. The Rinascente destroyed. Who knows how much money was lost!... And after work—he whispered, taking advantage of the fact that Sandie had left to serve dessert—*to the brothel! To satisfy the urges! Here, in Milan, all brothels were five and ten lire, there wasn't just a single one or two. Everything was regulated, all the whores carried identification. There were medical exams once a month that the nurses gave in the hospital! It wasn't how it is nowadays. Now you see them actually walking around the street, mixing with decent people. If we went to the brothel back then, it was because we were well educated and didn't want to do such things to girls from good families*—he looked into my eyes—*do you understand me? It was very different from these modern times. You see, if brothels are prohibited, young men won't learn the difference between an honest woman and a whore. There are still some good places, of course, if you know where to look ...*

—

Sandie came back with a tiramisu. She didn't pretend to have prepared it herself. The dessert was the exact opposite of Sandie: a perfect balance of flavors, layers, and the vanilla arriving at just the right moment of our intoxication.

Sandie's father retired from the dining table after eating his dessert. Before leaving, he put his card in my pocket with the address of a brothel and gave me a warning sign by putting his index finger on his lower eyelid, leaning over and whispering in my ear: *—Don't worry if you have no money. Just say you're with Commander Mellein, show them my card, and they'll put it on my account.*

When we were alone, Sandie invited me to her study. For the third time, the decoration changed radically; it was as if I had entered three different houses on the same night. The sofa and furniture had curved wooden arms and thin legs with brass cuffs. The upholstery was plastic, an artificial green with white stripes.

—Was your father very active during Fascism?

—More or less. You would have also gone along. It was the motherland against the foreigners. Your life or mine.

—But Mussolini was a sadist, an irrationalist.

—Why are you so interested in Mussolini? Are you stupid? I wasn't even alive then. People are always hurt in war.

—I'm interested in people who do harm, because I hate them. It's natural.

—Then you're in trouble. You must hate everyone. Mussolini isn't hurting you now. All of dad's speeches about the painting? Mom had a few authentic works, but the rest he added after she died. Most of them are fakes. He was messing with you!

She lit a cigarette, throwing the match into an ashtray that was also a battery-operated radio.

—You worry about too many things. You have to focus. You have to make your mind a spiritual reflector. That's how you can channel all your energy into a single cosmic direction and achieve harmony ... Wait a second, I'm going to show you what I bought today!

She threw her shoes into the air, ran barefoot to her bedroom, and came back wearing a pair of pink furry sandals that showed her toenails painted fuchsia. The sandals had red lights on the toes.

—I got them so I don't trip when I get up at night. Check it out! —and she turned off the light.

These little lights became the center of the world. Sandie ran to the turntable and played a Rita Pavone record, then she came back to the sofa. I sat in front of her, two steps away. When she put her feet on the sofa, the sandals lit the knees of my pants.

—Look, politics is the outside world, where men are most at ease. If you want to be a Christian or a socialist, that is fine by me, as long as you don't become a communist. Anything but that! As for me, I am content with feminine functioning, which is the inner world, the spirit, where I feel most comfortable. The feminine can never be fully known. Only women can intuit it, in our dreams, and when we discuss them with our therapists.

She turned her foot slightly and the red glow slid across my trousers until it stopped at the crotch.

—You lack calm, balance. I read in a magazine about an exercise for couples that helps them create harmony with the cosmos.

She sat on the carpet and her sandals pointed toward the fake white chimney and a vase on the mantel, which contained a plant with a few pointed leaves, more like twisted sabers than vegetation.

—Come, sit next to me, back-to-back. You have to understand that you are the outer principle and I the inner feminine.

You have to think that we are one, and because we are, we don't need to try to comprehend each other.

—Sure ... but not with Rita Pavone.

She changed the cheesy music, and we sat on the floor, back-to-back.

—Besides, why are you so concerned with what my father says. He is a good person, you know; you just have to say the right things, and he'll give you whatever you want. There is not an ounce of stupidity in him, and he's a lynx when it comes to *business*. Although he does have this thing with Mussolini. Is your Oedipus complex not resolved? You know what that is, right? It's when you hate your parent of the same sex. This song "*Tutta tua*" says it very clearly: the son is interested in his father; then he wants to take his place in everything, even in bed, because the father is his ideal. Are you following me? She touched my shoulder, so I turned to face her.

—I know what an Oedipus complex is, but no, I don't think I have that; in my case ...

—Everyone has it ...

Her head moved dangerously toward me.

—Not me. Sandie, you are a decent girl and I can't betray your father like this under his own roof. I respect you and I like you, I would even marry you, but I don't know what is going to become of me, or if I would even be able to offer you the kind of life you deserve, to buy you these beautiful sandals, this ashtray radio ... The fact is that my family will be bankrupt after my mother's treatment—and I am not a lynx for business ... I left and never saw her again.

VI

AT THE END OF March of 1966, the doctors concluded the flap had taken. They decided to take off the orthopedic devices and the immense cast that held the arm next to the chin. From that point on, the surgeries went as well as one could expect, considering that the goal was to distribute the new matter as well as possible.

We took advantage of this improvement, and Eligia was able to start walking again after so many months. During our short excursions through the corridors, the groups of big noses looked at us horrified as they waited nervously for their turn under the scalpel. When Eligia gained more strength, I decided to make a visit we had promised a while ago. One Sunday morning, very early, we went to the clinic's chapel, a modern space with joyful stained-glass windows and bright, stylized altars. We sat in a far corner where the officiant wouldn't be able to see us. There were few parishioners. All nurses or maids. The same priest who had come to Eligia's room was leading the service with the same intensity I remembered; he glanced at the girls with a look of astonishment and delivered his sermon.

—

—Let's make good use of this early service, as no patients are here with us. Today we can talk about the issues that are of particular interest to all of you young women. You are single and far from your homes, and this city is full of temptations. I will now tell you about the temptations of the flesh. You are creatures in a dangerous situation, abandoned to your own devices … This is precisely the first meaning of the word "flesh": that of a creature that has been abandoned by God. It is already clear in John: "It is the Spirit who gives life; the flesh profits nothing."

Two maids were whispering in the row ahead of us.

—Where did you go last night?

—To the movies. I went to see a film with Paul Newman.

—Which one?

—*The Prize*. It's about a writer who gets drunk.

—How was it?

—Some bad people want to kill him, because, somehow, he got in their way. He denounces a conspiracy inside the secret service, but no one believes him! That little mouth spouting insults and kisses at the same time. Anyways, they throw him into the water when a freighter is passing! I wasn't paying close attention because I had company … Paul Newman always looks like someone who doesn't know what he's about to do. That boxer's nose next to those baby eyes. Hmmm!… I love it! Do you think I have an Oedipus complex with Paul Newman?… No! How can I have that!

—… But beyond this first state—that of "living matter abandoned by the hand of God"—there is an even worse one. We no longer find

the abandoned, but what has been possessed by the desire for immediate pleasure: not indifferent to the spirit, but opposed to it, an instrument of the Devil. That is why Paul speaks of the need to enslave and punish the flesh: "I discipline my body and make it my slave ..."

—I don't understand this part of the sermon —I said to Eligia— what immediate pleasure is he talking about?

—He expresses himself well, with spontaneity. It's evident he took the humanities seriously.

—And did you go to the movies with Esteban? —the same maid asked her friend.

—Yes, but he is no Paul Newman.

—Did he touch you?

—A little.

—Don't play prude with me. Tell me everything!

—*... But we shouldn't exercise the kind of discipline that seeks to destroy or deny it. No, I'm talking about the discipline to reconquer and* transfigure *the flesh, so it can advance into a positive spiritual state ...*

— ... and then he gave me a portable radio so small I can practically take it anywhere: in my purse, my bra; now I can listen to music while I work ...

— ... wait, what bra size are you?

— *... Transfigured, the flesh is predisposed to the joy of God. It is*—the priest's voice rose and hesitated indecisively, before returning to its normal tone, as if it had suddenly regretted where it was going—*... it transforms into an instrument of good will, for helping others, which is particularly important for all of you, who have chosen a humanitarian profession. It is no longer the flesh against the spirit, but the flesh extending a hand to help a neighbor, and, through the needy, it helps its own spirit ...*

—That is exactly what I think! —I mumbled to myself.

— … Think about your daily life, about all those lost hours in a movie theater or in front of a television, hours in which your flesh "profits nothing," as John says, and that is if you're watching something good; if you're watching something bad, your flesh turns evil, "with a desire for pleasure," as Paul says; that's what occurs when you watch those shows created by the Devil or the communists. Do away with that screen of perdition! There is more to life on the other side. The screen is a like a shroud hiding your own skull and remains. You will be buried there at the end of an idle life that is wasted on those deceptive and tempting images: behold your own cadaver, rotting behind the screen, you're just like those dead bodies you have to remove from these rooms, flesh that is indifferent to God, until the Final Judgment can restore it. It is only by accepting God's offer that you can reconcile the flesh and spirit. In the words of a saint: "We exult in God through our Lord Jesus Christ, through whom we have now been reconciled."

—I don't remember my bra size. Also, I left it at Esteban's. Anyways, it's smaller than Elke Sommer's, I assure you. What did Paul Newman see in that German?

— … Therefore, it is only through discipline that you will be able to tame the flesh, and once it is dominated, you will also conquer the fear of death, you will be the master of your dusty bones. You will finally trick death, which so frightens you now when it takes a patient. I will let you into a little secret: all those artists whose work you see in churches, images representing terrible, frightening deaths that shake viewers to the core—from the highest clerics to the peasant—are not true Christians …

—They are savages, irrationalists —I whispered into Eligia's ear. She had never been interested in art.

— … For the true Christian, who has tamed the flesh, death is but a passing cold, or an unprotected child who tries to scare his

elders. The chosen ones don't die, for they have freed themselves from fear and know that the only thing that is mortal is death itself. Take pity on her, the putrefaction of the flesh, her deceitful and provisional bones!

—Wait, I didn't hear what he said ... I haven't been paying attention. What if we're asked what the Father said?

—He said we must do a good job cleaning the room after a patient dies. C'mon, let's go. We're going to be late. This just keeps going on and on.

After a few minutes, almost all the parishioners were leaving to begin their work shifts. The sermon had gone on for too long, and the chapel had slowly begun to empty as the priest looked around incredulously. He concentrated with his usual gesture, closing his eyes tightly and pressing his jaw to his chest; then he opened them wide and said in a low but determined voice: *—Well then, blame me again now!* On that furious note, he resumed:

—We were not made to fit the mold of death, but the mold of love, of that flesh the Son incarnated to show His infinite love. What a wonder! Someone who, at last, instead of exercising all his power, deliberatively imposed limits on it. This is "kenosis"—the voluntary renunciation of His divine nature for us to bear our sins—similar to how in the Old Testament, Yahweh makes himself small in order to make room for man and give him freedom ...

—So I guess the man knows Greek, too. I'm envious!—I exclaimed.

— ... This is the model: we must love as much as we have been loved. In His bosom, that is, in His love, "as much" means "infinite." It is up to us to maintain. "How?" we may ask ourselves. The answer is in the Old Testament: if you offer unconditional love to someone who doesn't deserve it, sooner or later, your tre-

mendous love will transform that person into someone worthy of it. "Love"—a word so abused in those popular songs—that is the word, not "money," not "war" or "destruction," as the lords of the world believe …

—What horror, so much violence! —said Eligia with quiet conviction.

—*… This is the interpretation of love, according to the prophet: "For I am God and not man, the Holy One in your midst. And I will not come in wrath." During the Vatican Council we see many changes, but these words don't change; take the word of this insignificant man.*

He repeated his usual gesture of deep concentration, then he looked around disoriented.

—*We will end up learning this lesson … whether we like it or not …* He hesitated for a second, before continuing in a more joyous tone. —*In these words we will find each other, sooner or later, and if there are no words left, we will do so in the crucified body that bared itself so we could reconcile in its caress …*

—

Toward the end of spring, Professor Calcaterra began touching Eligia's face very carefully, especially the fleshy right cheek. I sensed a subtle hesitation or disappointment in the movement of his fingers. Eligia asked him when they were going to cover those wells, and the professor answered evasively.

—There are some hypertrophic scars … We will see.

Our doctor had several ways of analyzing the wounds: he scraped them, applying a crystal to the most congested zones; but mostly he relied on his touch. One day, he finally brought himself to say what he had been thinking: a second flap was required, they still didn't have enough to work with. Eligia did not say anything. I tried to be encouraging, assuring her that getting more "material" was precisely what was needed for the perfect job, and reminding her that she had already endured too much to back down at this point. The truth is that Eligia hadn't shown any signs of backing down or becoming discouraged, not even when the doctor broke the news. She simply hadn't spoken.

That night I drank too much. Dina asked me to come with her to a job. Some clients had phoned her. Good, well-known guys, she said.

—So why do you want me to go with you then?

—You're my friend, and you're not looking too good. I don't want to leave you alone.

—Who says I'm not feeling well? Stop your stupid diagnoses.

—Come on! They have a bar with all types of whiskey.

We walked through an area of the city with old construction. There were none of the shiny, clear surfaces that abound in Rome. Dina searched in her purse and took out a key ring with inscribed golden initials. We opened a large dark portal and went in. The passageway was mostly dark, but I could see a faint light in the distance. It could easily have fit two cars. We walked in silence to the end and turned left. Dina flicked a switch and a bright light came on, illuminating a huge window and a delightful garden, the exact opposite of what I was expecting. Nothing in the exterior or the entryway anticipated this lush, green corner.

The architecture enclosing the small garden looked heavy and menacing, but the heathers, junipers, blueberries, the purple rhododendrons and the little ash tree at the center, were arranged playfully, and also impeccably. Since it was spring, they remained in a dormant state, reserving their exuberance for summer. This urban flora, so civilized, so prudent, existed collectively in forms and adaptations that allowed different species to complement each other. The blueberry plants, pressing softly against some of the austere junipers, were shown their way to freedom; the rhododendrons surrounded the ash tree with their intense colors. This wise configuration of colors and forms created a harmonious space much larger than what a geometrist would call "real," or having perspective. The sense of space created by this little garden was the product of collaboration, of each plant consulting its neighbor and the whole as it blossomed. I was hypnotized, trying to remember what I had done wrong.

The apartment turned out to be the lion's den of two newly rich industrialists; it was decorated with violet, pink, fuchsia, and salmon colors. The men were no more than forty.

—Don't you have a tie? —asked the younger of the two, a few minutes after Dina introduced us (to them: "he's my cousin, he had one drink too many tonight"; to me: "they are old clients, trusted friends").

—Do you want one? Just pick one out, there are several in the closet. Then go buy us some food —he said and handed me a huge bill, almost a sheet. —There is a good restaurant around the corner of Via Spartaco. I want a meat dish, a stuffed chop or something like that.

—Is it very far?

—Why? You don't have a car? Here, take my keys. I have two. What are you waiting for?

—I don't know how to drive.

—Dammit! —my new, magnanimous friend snapped at me.

Dina laughed, and the other man looked annoyed.

—Then take a cab —he said, handing me another bill.

As I was leaving, Dina said to me with a smile: —Don't take it personally, it's the economic miracle that makes them behave like that.

When I returned, there was no one in the living room, and I could hear a creaking sound coming from the bedroom. Their bar was poorly stocked. They had some Italian and French bottles, but no Scotch. I was already drinking when Dina came out of the room and locked herself in the bathroom. The younger man asked me for his food, and I pointed to a package in the kitchen.

—Warm it up and make yourself a plate too. You don't look too good.

The four of us sat to eat in the kitchen. The food was a crime: *milanesas de costeletas*, stuffed with bread crumbs, ham, and cheese melting over the edges and forming a pool of doughy milk next to the fried apples that served as garnish. The meat had almost disappeared in all those sauces and fried crap. When cut, it dripped molten cheese instead of simple blood. You might as well have been eating an alien instead of a cow. I missed the steaks from my country.

—Are you bored? —Dina had asked when she entered the kitchen.

—No, but they don't have Scotch, as you promised.

—Liar! You promised me the best for my cousin —Dina said to the younger of the men.

—We probably finished it—he said—what do I know.

—Now you get in your second car and go buy us a bottle of Scotch.

The man hesitated for a second, but then got up. His friend grabbed his arm.

—What the hell are you doing? Are you crazy? You're going to take orders from a whore?

—What did you think... that I was going to do as she says? — replied the other with a forced laugh. —Ah! No whiskey for the little prince—he said with a mocking and defiant tone.

—Oh yeah? Then we're leaving.

—By all means, go with that bum —the older man said with disgust.

Dina went to the room and finished dressing slowly, giving them time to reconsider. In the kitchen, the older man remained still, and the younger one, looking annoyed, whispered—... she's pretty hot...

I was trying to drink as much wine as possible from the bottle they had opened.

—Hey, slowly! —shouted the young one. —Think about the rest of us!

Dina returned fully dressed.

—Very well, I'm leaving now, so pay me.

—My ass we'll pay—said the older man. The deal was for the entire night.

—Listen, I did what I had to do. Now I want my money... This is what happens when you trust old clients.

The younger man got up and opened the front door.

—Get out then!

Dina stared intently at him, while the other repeated:

—Are you deaf? Leave!

—I'm not leaving until I get paid.

The younger man got up calmly and grabbed Dina by the hair.

She twisted and turned, sobbing, hitting him and scratching his face as he dragged her all the way to the lobby. I walked to where they were and then we heard the door slam behind us.

—Did they hurt you?

—No—I said.

We decided to go into the garden. It was hard to see the entrance, so Dina switched on the light by the main gate, giving us just enough time to walk to the green before it turned off again.

—I definitely left a mark on his face ... and I didn't leave empty-handed.

She opened her purse and took out a porcelain statuette of a 1920s bather, standing with a large, light-blue towel and wearing a bathing suit with an overskirt. It was utterly hideous.

—Do you like it?

—No.

—I wonder how much it would sell for?—she said.

—Nothing.

—So you're also an antiquarian?

—You don't have to be one to see this thing is worthless.

—It must be worth something ...

—It's worth nothing ... You're a disaster when it comes to business.

The statuette wobbled in Dina's hands. She placed it on top of a fountain attached to the wall. The fountain was in the shape of a shell, and a lion's head spat out a trickle of water. The statuette displaced a small volume of the water, which splashed the ground with a thud. The trickling sound eventually came to resemble a ticking clock. Dina wet her hands and ran them through my hair. The cooling sensation had the effect of a blood transfusion. The touch of this timid but effective water calmed the turbulence in my blood.

—Ok then —said Dina— I'm off, bye-bye. Hang in there, you're strong.

—Where are you going?

—Back to those two. I need the money, and, believe it or not, they need me.

—Goodbye—I said.

My meetings with Dina filled a quota of unpredictability that helped compensate for the routine of the clinic. They also provided a temporary relief from the uncertainties of Eligia's treatment. I often caught myself staring at the color of a skin graft and trying to remember its previous coloration in order to deduce—based on the slightest difference—whether there had been any progress. But it is very difficult to remember a specific shade of color; tones exist in the present. The constant study of that skin made me feel uneasy: at times, I believed there was favorable progress; and at other times, the necrosis seemed unstoppable. I would have gone mad, but Eligia had the virtue of quietly generating life in any circumstance; the grafts germinated anywhere they placed them. But my disbelief persisted, and I looked with apprehension at the natural secretions of the wounds at both ends of the new flap, as if each of them throbbed with the threat of infection. That matter, in transit from her arm to her face, also carried all my hopes.

When it came time to give Eligia food (I wouldn't call it lunch or dinner because these were not ordinary dishes, but generous servings of a thick liquid with an indefinable color), her situation seemed like that of a child, almost to a ridiculous point. To protect the grafts, I had to cover her with several bibs.

Eligia could not chew, because her jaw had limited mobility, and the doctors had advised her not to try, as it could damage the flap; so she settled for sucking the warm, yellowish liquid. My job was to bring the soup close to her mouth and make sure no lumps obstructed the straw: a simple job, though it required some concentration. The bowl had to be held five centimeters away from her face and the second cast, which immobilized the opposite arm.

All these tedious precautions were forgotten at night, with the possibility that anything could happen. At the time, it seemed to me that the only poor echo of my labors were the praises of the nurses and maids—though they were mostly sarcastic, since my work meant less money for them. "How brave, always next to her," they said. It is also true that, whenever she could, Eligia would intertwine her fingers with mine if my hand passed close to hers.

My abrupt and unexpected excursions at night had become the only way to mark the passage of time in that foggy city. Nights when I couldn't find Dina simply did not register in my memory. I would just return to the room, search my pockets to make sure I hadn't lost anything, and feel proud when I found no emotions, only emptiness.

I lived in two spheres: the one that revolved around Eligia and the one that revolved around Dina; both were close in space and time, but isolated from each other. The nocturnal—as I thought back then—was separated from any project linked to my life. The sphere of Eligia's wounds would bind me forever; Dina's, on the other hand, would inevitably disappear any moment I chose.

VII

ONE DAY, CLOSE TO the holiday Ferragosto, when the city seemed deserted, Dina came into the bar and asked if I wanted to come with her and a client to a cabaret that was kind of far, but very fun.

—You'll see, you will like it —said the client, who wore a shirt with white and blue vertical stripes, and seemed interested in taking as many people as possible to this place.

—All right, but don't forget—I responded, turning to Dina. —I have to return to the clinic before Eligia wakes up so I can give her breakfast.

We arrived at San Silvestro and saw a large poster on the façade: "A special night dedicated to Milan fans ... and as usual, a great celebration of the New Year!" A stocky woman employee gave us whistles, rattles, and little plastic trumpets as we entered; she concluded her welcoming ritual by blowing her own wind instrument in our faces, crowning us with little hats displaying the colors of the Milan team (white and a blue that was almost black).

The place was very crowded, considering that the city was almost empty during the summer holidays. The fact that tourist agencies barely mentioned Milan in their itineraries—perhaps a few hours to see the Duomo and the Galleria—meant that its most delicate secrets were preserved for the *happy few*. There wasn't a single tourist in sight at San Silvestro; just a bunch of Italians having fun. Almost every man had paired with some girl from the venue, and everyone wore the little white-and-blue hats. Loud whistles and rattles filled the air, completely out of sync with the songs that played from the loudspeakers.

Dina leaned on the bar with her characteristic gesture, rounding her shoulders and lowering her head. They poured us two glasses of cheap, sour champagne. Meanwhile, the client in the striped shirt greeted everyone as if he were an old regular. After that, he busied himself whispering things in Dina's ear. Suddenly, the music stopped, and an enthusiastic, sexless voice announced over the loudspeaker: *"It's already eleven! In one hour we will celebrate the New Year! Get ready for the party! Forget your problems! Tonight, we celebrate the year from August to August! Farewell, stupid year! So long, taxes and politicians, and—not least—so long, wives!"* A general euphoria with a loud roar of cheers and whistles welcomed these last three words.

The voice continued with its words of false joy, but soon a malfunction produced a ghostly electric buzz around some low-pitched sounds: *"The San Silvestro is the only place where you are safe from evil, and also from Inter fans. Here, tonight, everything is Milan, everything is white and blue, nothing is red and black! Beautiful women and guaranteed joy. Champagne for everyone. Who cares about tomorrow, tomorrow is the first day of the rest of our lives! What's more, if you want, you can come back tomorrow and celebrate another New Year with us! The fifteenth, out of respect for the Holy Madonnina, we'll be closed. But any night that isn't a religious holiday is a party at San Silvestro. Every night welcomes a New Year!"*

I must admit that the women and men that worked at that place did a good job. They seemed to actually be enjoying themselves ... and why wouldn't they? This job was a good one, as long as the customers were in the right mood. Their routine must have been tougher during the winter, with many fewer clients, numb from the cold or without enough money, the women pretending to be happy in that void, and sounding their pathetic plastic trumpets as they danced in place to keep warm. But on this summer night, the euphoria kept rising as twelve o'clock approached. The waiters kept laughing and filling the glasses with that frothy acid. They made sure everyone could hear the corks shooting out of the bottles. The bartender let out a yell when that happened, and sounded a bell hanging from the ceiling. Everyone scrambled to catch the flying cork, because San Silvestro gave a free drink to whoever found it; having the customers crawl under the tables looking for the thing also provided a good opportunity to pick their pockets. Then, if someone realized his wallet was missing, all the women and waiters began a frantic search, while mumbling: "The short one who left in a hurry just a minute ago definitely looked like a thief."

The bartender poured me a drink. After asking me where I was from, he burst into laughter:

—South American! Like Sívori! The best football player in the world! Now, how is it possible that you have such good players but horrible teams? ... Independiente not only loses against Milan, they even lose against Inter ...

I was in the mood for teasing, and I also didn't want any problems. Anything Dina could offer seemed small compared to this abundance of women, New Year's, and champagne. The ladies kept saying I could take them to any dark corner for a few lire. They came from everywhere in Italy and there were also foreigners from other continents, including Oceania. I had never been with someone from Africa or Asia. For a few coins, I could say—without lying and for the rest of my life—that I had been with women from all latitudes of the globe.

Milan offered real abundance; one could be hypnotized by all aspects of squandering, which in San Silvestro were easily within reach: party hats, plastic trumpets, women of unusual features, and more. But giving in to these "trinkets" also demanded, of course, letting go of any idea of organization: this requirement was also the prize.

Suddenly, the music stopped, and the master of ceremonies asked that everyone be quiet. The lights went out, some female hands slid into men's pockets, and the androgynous voice coming from the half-functioning speakers shrieked: —*Silence! Only forty seconds till the end of the year!... Thirty, twenty-nine, twenty-eight ... So long, dirty year! Take all your misfortunes with you!... Twenty, nineteen, eighteen ... This year will be better, you'll see, you fucking year, what a good run we'll have! Good business, iron health, real women! Five ... four ... three ... two ... one ... And here we go! Happy New Year!*

All the lights flashed and confetti fell. People blew their

little trumpets. Through the clouds of artificial smoke, I saw Dina at the other end of the bar in her bright summer dress, looking bored and staring at the ceiling.

A couple of hours later, a group of men entered San Silvestro. Among them was a large, muscular man with a buzzed head and a big face that exuded laughter and sweat. It was obvious they had been drinking. The big one sat on a stool close to me and asked for vermouth. It was two in the morning. The bartender said he didn't have any, but when the man mentioned he would happily pay the same price as for champagne, a bottle of vermouth magically appeared. Mr. Big-face was chatty and exuberant. Two women came and sat next to him. He continued drinking his vermouths, and they ordered more of the house champagne.

The youngest prostitute at the cabaret—who also happened to be the most attractive—stared at him intently from afar. She was sitting with an older man with white hair and a tie, who seemed quite wealthy and was also very drunk. Half an hour later, she walked toward the *toilette*, and made a point of passing by my neighbor who kept drinking vermouth.

Just as he had done with every woman within earshot, he screamed some vulgarity at this young lady. She stopped a short distance away and stared back at him. Vermouth man was smitten. The young woman glanced at the sofa where the old tycoon was waiting for her while taking advantage of her absence to chat with the prostitute on the next couch.

—Do you know who I am?—she asked.

Big-face thought about it for a second.

—No—he said.

—Are you sure?

At that exact moment, the tycoon realized what was happening and started stumbling toward the bar. His shoes were gray, shiny, and very tapered. Anticipating a brawl, a bunch of other men in white-and-blue hats began to gather behind him. Those who had arrived with Big-face flanked him, and yelled —To us! The ones from old Ambrosiana, the guard of Viale Goethe!

It was then that I noticed they were all dressed in red and black. The two groups were lined up on either side of the dance floor. White-and-blue versus red-and-black. The tycoon pointed at the young woman and yelled:

—You! Come here!

—I can't. I have to talk with this man—she said, pointing to the large, sweaty face, which now appeared slightly terrified.

The tycoon charged toward her, but halfway there—and this could have been on account of his new pointy shoes, the freshly waxed dance floor, or the fact that he was completely wasted—he slipped and fell in a split. His friends in the white-and-blue hats didn't move, but, at that moment, a thin gentleman in a blazer and a tie—which looked quite similar to those sported by the men in red-and-black—made his way through the crowd toward the center of the dance floor. He tried to help the tycoon get back on his feet, and whispered in his ear:

—Have you seen anything like this before, commander?

He tried to pick him up three times, but the Caesar-like millionaire kept falling. The red-and-black team started to walk over with curiosity, and the thin gentleman turned pale once he saw what was upon him. Suddenly, he grabbed the tycoon by the collar and yelled:

—You piece of shit! What a mess you got us in! You're on your own.

Propelled forward, the red-and-black team passed over the tycoon and surrounded the thin gentleman. Contrary to what we all expected, they didn't put a hand on him. The young prostitute didn't flinch when she saw Big-pockets on the floor, but his friends, who were more numerous than the red-and-blacks, finally reacted. Both groups started breaking bottles to use as weapons. Some advanced and others backed down, then, for unexplained reasons, the situation reversed and those who had backed down started moving forward. Finally, one of the red-and-blacks yelled: —We're outnumbered!, and that was enough for the whole group to retreat while yelling *We'll meet again at San Siro!*

The customers in the white-and-blue hats didn't even notice they had won because the waiters, to stop things from escalating, had released more confetti and turned on the smoke machines. Only when the smoke began to clear did they realize their victory. They were already raising brandy shots for toasts when someone yelled: —The Inters have brought reinforcements!, and, just like that, everyone was gone.

Once the place was almost empty, a few customers, who had nothing to do with football, came in. Surprised, they asked the bartender why there were so few customers. The bartender made an exaggerated gesture and said: —There was a fight here, I can't even begin to tell you!

And thus, the night of August 13, 1966, became history and legend.

The event would most certainly reach mythological status in just a few nights—but the immediate effect of that remark was to scare the newcomers. As soon as they saw three men in red and black come in (they were drunk, lost, looking for a pay phone), they decided to get the hell out of there as fast as possible. The thin gentleman, who had come to the aid of the old tycoon, quickly turned into the "connoisseur of the night" and offered to help the three men find their phone booth.

The only people left were the waiters, Dina, her client, the young woman, Mr. Big-face, and yours truly.

— . . . so you still don't know who I am?

—No . . . I don't . . .

—I'm your daughter.

—Ana?! . . . How many years . . . Ana, of course!

—Yes, how many years!

—If you only knew how much I've thought about you and wanted to see you.

—No, I don't know.

For a moment the air tightened around them, but soon she relaxed and kissed him on the cheek. The man was overjoyed. He put his arms around her, and after they spoke for a few minutes in low voices, he yelled at the top of his voice:

—This is extraordinary! We must celebrate . . . vermouth for everyone! It's on me.

There was barely anyone left in the cabaret. The three bottles he had opened were at arm's length, so I drank and drank, while Big-face gave me the evil eye. Finally, he exploded:

—I invited everyone, and you're drinking all of it!

—This isn't a place for cheapos.—I said.

Mr. Greasy Sweat hesitated for a second, looked at his daughter, and then grabbed the collar of my old black coat and started shaking me like a bell. I reached into my pocket for the stewardess's knife, and clutched it, but my hand froze.

The more insults Big-face slurred at me, the heavier and more rigid my hand felt. I thought to myself: —Just take it out and the whole situation will change. But I didn't move my arm.

Around dawn, Dina and her friend took me to the car. I rested my head on the back seat, and as soon as we started moving, all of Milan turned into a merry-go-round. I begged them to stop, got out, and sat on the sidewalk.

—You don't look well! Try to vomit. —said Dina's client.

—I won't succumb to cheap champagne and vermouth; it's not fair!

I had the urge to lie down but I didn't feel like vomiting. Back then, I never felt like vomiting.

—Why get drunk if your liver can't take it? Listen, I'm taking Dina to a hotel. We can't take you. You figure it out. She tells me you're used to it ...

The two of them left, and I crawled along the sidewalk until reaching a wall that could support my body.

The sun was just coming out when I opened my eyes again. Dina was shaking my shoulder. Finally, she lost her balance from laughing and fell on top of me. Behind her, two elderly women, one dressed in black, the other holding a rosary, stared at us in silence.

—C'mon. You have to make an effort; we need to go—said Dina.

When I sat up, she supported me with her shoulder and pulled me to my feet. She couldn't stop laughing. Her nonsense, plus the weight of my body, made it difficult to wave a taxi.

—Ok, lean on this and stay quiet —she pointed to a ledge on one of the walls.

The bricks on my back felt warm; it was a big improvement over the sidewalk. I put my hands to the side to keep from falling right or left, and Dina found this hilarious. She laughed so hard it became contagious and I started laughing too. It was exactly what I needed to start vomiting. I laughed and vomited in equal, alternate measures: a few good laughs and then three or four torrents from my Neptunian mouth. The waves of vomit corresponded to the number of laughs, and this was completely unintentional. The liquid was completely translucent; the vermouth and the champagne were intact. Dina tried to stop the vomit with her green neck scarf, but quickly gave up and left. I tried to follow her but fell asleep laughing.

Dina was next to me when I opened my eyes again. Behind her was a taxi with the back door open. I was no longer in a laughing mood and a heavy sleep weighed over me. I heard the driver say:

—And this little angel ... You didn't tell me about him.

He got out of the car, pulled me to my feet, and led me to the passenger seat.

—What a mess. He turned toward Dina, who had collapsed in the back seat. —You'll have to thank me later for this one.

We drove off. From time to time, the driver made a joke about my state, which always ended up with an observation about how good he was being to us and a glance at Dina with a smile. The taxi driver was right; he was being a good guy. I looked like hell.

—Who knows where you'd be right now. Do you have anybody who's responsible for you?

—He's a foreigner —said Dina in a low, tired voice.

—And you? Who takes care of you?

—I have an aunt.

—Ah! What a lucky aunt, with a nice niece like you.

The car was moving slowly. In my half sleep, I saw that he started driving off the road and into one of those empty lots between construction sites. The taxi driver stopped the car and moved to the back seat. I got out of the car to urinate and look at the buildings around. From the balconies and windows, a few people stared at us in the silence of dawn. Someone yelled something in the distance. I tried to zip up my trousers but after a few failed attempts threw myself back on the front seat. The car swayed gently, like a crib, while someone in the back seat moaned. I couldn't tell if it was a man's or a woman's voice. Later, I felt the taxi driver adjusting my position with a single hand:

—Stay seated, eh, I don't want you to fall—he said while his other hand patted my chest until he found what he was looking for.

He took out my wallet, kept the money, and put it back in my coat. He had stolen the two thousand lira I'd reserved for the only whore in San Silvestro who was from Polynesia. I wondered when I would get another opportunity to make love with a woman from that part of the world.

—I don't understand how you're not dying of heat in that coat.

Those were the last words the taxi driver said to me.

He gave the money to Dina, who was lying down half asleep. When we arrived at the clinic, the taxi driver made us get out.

—Well, you can manage now. I did my good deed. I'm not even charging you for the trip.

—Yeah … just imagine—answered Dina.

She put my arm around her shoulders so I wouldn't fall.

—What am I going to do with you? You're such a pain in the neck.

—Let go. I'll just go to my room.

Dina let go. I took two steps, and fell on all fours. She pulled me up again.

—Where is the guard?

—He's usually asleep in the bathroom this time of day. Why?

—Well, we'll have to go in. What a face you have! I can't leave you here like this. What is your room number?

—407—I said.

We waited until the coast was clear and went through the gate without anyone seeing us. Once inside, we took the elevator with one of the secretaries. In the corridor, we came across the maid from the morning shift.

—Mr. Mario, what happened to you?! An accident?

—No, I'm fine. How's she doing?

—Your mother is resting. You're hurt?

—Your mother! —said Dina outraged.—Can you take this baby here to bed?

—That is not my job—said the maid, whose cousin I had refused to hire for the night shift.—Why don't you put him to bed yourself? It's obvious you have experience. And you should close his fly while you're at it.

Leaning on Dina's arm, I opened her purse and took out two bills that smelled like the taxi driver's semen. I gave them to the maid and made a sign with my finger to keep this a secret. She thanked me.

Dina walked me to our room slowly. In my mind I was saying farewell to my beloved Polynesian. It was only when we got to the door that I remembered my room was also Eligia's.

—Shh—I said to Dina—don't make so much noise. I can manage from here.

I ended up slamming the door open without meaning to, and a lucid voice asked at once:

—Mario?

—I'm fine. I'm with someone who accompanied me here.

I took two steps into the vestibule, where the bed still remained out of sight. Then I put my hand on the wall and started sliding toward the floor. Eligia asked for me again. This time she sounded worried. Dina helped me up.

—I'm sorry, Madam. I didn't want to disturb you. Your son is ok. He only needs some sleep—she stammered, helping me through the vestibule.

When we reached the main room, Dina fell silent.

—Dina, this is Eligia. Eligia, this is Dina—I said. —Dina helped me a lot, although I didn't ask for it. I'm just in time to give you breakfast.

—I had breakfast an hour ago. Thank you, Dina.

I finally made it to my sofa bed, but Dina remained transfixed by the sight of Eligia. I noticed her arm had gone limp, so I let go of it and dropped to my little bed. Looking up, I saw Dina was still petrified, staring.

—Why are you still here! —I screamed.

She left without saying goodbye, more of an escape really ... I slept until the maid from the corridor came into the room as loudly as possible and shouted "The soup is here!" as she always did to save herself the trouble of gently waking up her patients.

I tried to prop myself up using my own strength.

—Are you managing, Mr. Mario? —asked the maid in a mischievous tone.

I recalled Eligia must have seen Dina, since the maid had refused to walk me to the room. The soup was thick and boiling. Before leaving, she pointed at my head:

—It looks very good on you. I'm also a Milan fan.

I took off the little hat. As I did four times a day, I carefully arranged several bibs around Eligia's mouth and under the bowl of soup, which I kept twenty centimeters from her face, the exact length of the straw. This was necessary in order to protect the precious new flesh gained from the second flap, the result of fifty days in the cast, between May and July.

Eligia stared at me intently. Once I finished feeding her, I returned to the sofa and said I would take a nap. My only concern was to hide my hangover.

It was almost dinnertime when I woke up again. I didn't feel well; my mouth was dry, though I noticed my legs had regained some strength. Eligia's eyes followed me everywhere. I washed her before dinner, trying to be extra attentive; I even suggested cutting her nails.

—No, not today ... but please, do something about your breath.

I brushed my teeth, and when I returned, she said:

—Do you remember when you made the Honor Roll in school?

—Ok, here we go again with the nostalgia—I said, trying to be funny.

A few minutes later, they brought another bowl of steaming soup and some jello. I arranged the bibs as usual and held the bowl with the straw close to her. It was very hot, so I blew on the surface. I also got an extra napkin to wipe any liquid that dripped from her mouth. That was the routine.

—Let's see, one sip for Piaget who is close by, in Geneva, riding a bicycle, and who will visit very soon ... Another for Herder ... Another for de Saussure ... Another for Dewey.

I forced a laugh. Eligia couldn't see the bowl so close to her mouth; a lump of something got stuck inside the straw. I shook it to the side with one hand, and the other began to tremble. I tried to control it, but the quivering grew, augmented by the weight of the bowl, then the flow of soup resumed.

—One sip for Professor Calcaterra, who was admitted to the Academy, and his photo is in all the important journals ...

The hand I had used to tap the straw quickly returned to its position under the bowl, but at that precise moment, I had a spasm and the liquid spilled all over the bibs and napkins, soaking Eligia. She screamed in pain. In between moans, she asked me to call the nurse. I pressed the emergency button. Not knowing what else to do, I tried to remove one of the steaming napkins from her face, but part of the skin graft was attached to it, revealing a mattress of raw tissue and blood. The nurse came in as I was screaming uncontrollably.

—It was an accident! The soup spilled!

—Mr. Mario! This is bad!

She acted quickly, unlocked the wheels, and ran with the bed to one of the treatment rooms. Everything happened in the blink of an eye. Closing my eyes, I sobbed with the soup bowl still in my hands. A few minutes later, still crying loudly, I said: —"I didn't mean for this to happen, Eligia! I just wanted to do good, I swear. This can't go on. If we get out of this one, I will change. I promise! I was sitting on my little bed.

Sometime later, I'm not sure how long, the nurse returned.

—Everything is under control—she said, looking me in the eyes—it wasn't that bad, you know. Everything will be ok. You can't give up now. She needs you more than ever. This kind of thing could have happened to anyone; after so many months. Everyone here is so impressed with how you take care of her! But it is true that, every so often, you should hire an extra nurse and take a break. It's just too much for a single person. I'm sure I can find you someone who isn't too expensive. Now go see your mother and take a dressing gown for her. If she starts to sneeze, we'll be in real trouble. Go, she's been asking for you. Give her a kiss.

When I entered the treatment room, I found Eligia's head placed on a metal counter next to a sink. She had no hair and was emaciated to a point I hadn't seen before; her eye sockets were empty and the bones were showing to varying degrees.

A compass-looking object was sticking out of her cheek, and on the dark, metallic counter, a goniometer provided a stark contrast with the cerulean colors of the head.

One of the professor's assistants came in from the main room, looked at me, and quickly put the instrument away.

—These models are very useful, you know. They allow us to plan the most complicated surgeries.

Eligia was surrounded by doctors. They had removed the damaged graft and covered it with a healing gauze pad. The doctors left orders for a new graft to be made in the morning. To the more than twenty surgeries, we now had to add this pointless one.

—Don't worry, Madam, it will only be a few minutes—said the doctor on call.

—How are you, Mario? —asked Eligia.

—I'm ok. I brought you a dressing gown. Do you want me to wait here or in the room?

—Go back to the room. They'll take good care of me. Try to get some rest.

I walked around the room for an hour. It looked so empty without the bed. Since the beginning of Eligia's treatment in Italy, I had never waited for her like this while she was in the operating room. I had always stayed close by in one of the waiting areas. This time, I moved aimlessly in the empty room. My feet had gotten used to moving around the bed, and all the new space now felt disorienting. I went to the spot where Eligia had been for months and looked at the room from her perspective. From that point of view, the space felt completely different. Most visible were the window and the Cézanne reproduction; the vestibule where Sandie, the priest, and Dina had come in was almost out of sight, as was my sofa bed against the other wall.

I tried to imagine what was happening in the treatment room. I considered all the possibilities; from the most pessimistic to the most hopeful. Without realizing it, I kept repeating to myself: —My God, what have I done.

The room recovered its logic when they brought back the bed.

—It was nothing, Mario—Eligia said.—Tomorrow they'll place another graft. It wasn't that good to begin with, and it's a small area. I have plenty of skin on my thigh.

She fell asleep soon after. A nurse came in quietly and took her pulse and temperature. She did not wake up. The night was just beginning.

—Everything is going well. Go get some fresh air. Just for tonight, we'll take care of her for free. Go distract yourself a little. Things like this happen when you've been inside too long.

This time I didn't go to the usual bar. I walked almost half a kilometer and reached a part of town where it was highly unlikely someone would recognize me. On a hidden street, I found a bar and drank half a dozen cognacs without anyone seeing me.

VIII

Ein Zeichen
kämmt es zusammen
zur Antwort auf eine grubelnde
Felskunst

(A sign
combs it together
as answer for a brooding rockart)

—Paul Celan
September, 1966

I MEET PLENTY OF idiots who regard me with envy because I travel alone. They think everything is so easy, that being young and traveling by yourself is the ultimate freedom. But the reality is quite different. The lone traveler is always at risk. Locals glance at you with suspicion, though, somehow, they always find a way to benefit from your presence: the hotel manicurist makes a little extra money or—surprise, surprise—a whore just happens to be sitting by herself in the cabaret at the end of the evening. Everything changes in places that aren't frequented by tourists: the lone traveler becomes an unusual threat, a Hun who broke away from the horde. But the truth is that he's more vulnerable than menacing. Mark my words: no matter how nice you are, no matter how much you say "yes," they will always try to cheat you: the whores, the waiters, the taxi drivers.

Traveling alone in this manner is like going to the movies or the theater by yourself. Now multiply that by a hundred. I know... I hate those idiots who won't even go around the corner by themselves. No one will convince me they believe in art. How lovely it all is—with the dialogue, the actors, the director, the play's message, the conversation at the bar afterward—but without someone there to hold their hand, some people won't even cross the street. With travel it's the same: an art gallery, a castle, everything is so beautiful, but people go only if they have someone; on their own they won't even leave their house.

So what the fuck am I doing here? What do I say to the locals in these small towns? How should I try to explain? That Eligia, after the success of her second flap, left for Geneva, and is now completely infatuated with Piaget? That the money I had set aside to travel for over a month disappeared in just three days of whiskey and a Polynesian whore? That I have no place to return, because the clinic already emptied our room, and we don't have it reserved again until the end of the month? That the only thing of value I have left is a *circolare*, a monthly pass that allows me to travel second class in any train? That for over twenty days I have been sleeping in trains and drinking the cheapest stuff I can find? That—given how long and narrow

Italy is—I have to spend a day in the south and a day in the north just to get my sleep in the train and save on the hotel? I start my day by getting off in some random little village, whatever the first stop is after I wake up. (Second-class stops in all the damn little villages.) I find a bar, wash my face, drink a few grappas, and start walking around a place whose name I haven't even bothered to remember. Inevitably, always—and I mean always—my path intersects with some marvelous work that can't be found in any art history book. It appears spontaneously around a corner, giving me no chance to anticipate if it will be Risorgimento, neoclassical, baroque, Renaissance, Gothic, Romantic, classical, or Etruscan. What can I say to these fools who are surrounded by pure wonders and don't even know it?

And what could I tell them about themselves? That during our talks in the train I have learned to substitute my paternal last name with that of my Italian great-grandfather? That as soon as they ask "Presotto, Mario, native?" and I answer "native," everyone wants to know if I'm related to this or that cousin? When it's time for dinner, the paninis and wine come out, and my new last name pays off. Without exception, I will kiss the hand that offers me a panini and a bottle of red wine. Thanks to that dependable hand, I'm still standing.

I had been walking through these streets of who-knows-where for over half an hour. In front of a small plaza—smaller than that garden in Milan—there was a huge church. I was tired so I decided to go in and sit on one of the benches. That morning I'd had too much grappa; a group of workers waiting to start their shift was very generous and treated me to a few rounds: —Look at our native friend in his coat! And it's still summer!

I leaned forward until my head was touching my knees. I put my hands on the back of my neck and pressed my head upward so the blood could return to my brain.

A priest came over.

—You can't stay here, this choir bench is reserved for the acolytes in the next Mass.

—That's fine, Father.

—You're not planning to beg here, right? You can only do that by the entrance; but you're too young. You still don't have that look of defeat. That's what really counts, more than the shabby clothes and the pallor ... —If you want to eat, come with me to the sacristy.

—No, that's not necessary—I said. —I'll stay quiet for a few minutes on this bench, and then I'll go for some fresh air.

—Yes, that will do you good.

I recovered; my loneliness felt heavy. Ten minutes went by. An older tourist couple approached. They were dressed modestly and in dark colors, no sandals with socks or Hawaiian shirts. The man gave me a dollar, and I put it in my coat.

—Excuse me, do you speak English? —he asked.

—A little.

—Can you translate this beautiful headstone for us?

—I can try—I said ... —Let's see ... Bishop Alessandro ... it's hard to read ... Here ... a date ... September 6, 1266. A good time to die, especially for bishops and merchants that could pay for a headstone like this.

—It's very beautiful.

—Yes. Those were the times of simple graves.—I felt the need to speak and let loose. —A horizontal statue, made to look as natural as possible, an idealized dead body. The figure isn't meant to represent the one who lived, but the one who will be resurrected, a perfect body for a perfect world. Look at the pedestal with saints in bas-relief: an old conservative, this Alessandro; instead, he could have preferred little angels inspired by these ancient times, something very fine and avant-garde. As you can see, there is nothing threatening in this tomb. In the 1200s, tombs were like second mothers, places to protect the body so it could be reborn fresh and without sins, a perfect symmetry with birth. It was only later, with the Counter-Reformation, that tombs began to feature dark concavities, skeletons, and skulls. But, you know, it is very curious, the scarier they tried to make them look in the 1600s ... the more luxurious they were built, with more marble and onyx on display, more *putti*.

—This is all very interesting! How do you know about these things? —the man asked.

—Well ... On some previous trip ... I remember my parents had a very good tourist guide. It must be still in my head somewhere with all the notes they took.

—Are you Italian?

—I'm South American. My name is Mario. How about you?

—We're Australian. I'm Charles, and this is my wife Sarah ... Is there a cemetery in this village?

—I think so. Why do you ask? Perhaps you share my opinion. If you want to know an Italian city: look for the cathedral, the plaza, and the brothel; but if you want to know a village ... the cemetery, the market, and a single whore will do!

—Perhaps you could come ... would you like to accompany us?

—To see the whore or the cemetery?

—No ... not at my age! The cemetery, of course ... I'm married!

Sarah laughed and continued scrutinizing Alessandro's tomb. The old couple exuded dignity and honesty.

—I guess I could—I said.

—We saw you speaking Italian with a priest just a few moments ago.

—Do they speak Italian in South America? —asked Sarah.

—No, but my mother's family is Italian.

—Ah, yes! Immigrants. We also have a lot of Italian immigrants back home ... Are you married? ... Do you have a girlfriend?

—No.

—Why not? —she asked.

—I didn't have good examples.

While Sarah told me about how wonderful their hotel was, her husband took a few photos of the Bishop Alessandro's tomb. I was happy to meet a tourist who was actually interested in what he was seeing.

—Before going to the cemetery, can we take a look at that tomb over there? —the old man asked, pointing his camera two chapels ahead.

It was a strange church, the kind you would expect to find in a big city. There were some Romanesque structures, and on the walls, above the side arches, small fragments of medieval frescoes rediscovered and restored, incomprehensible, and insignificant; an arm, a face, a truncated scene were scattered over the otherwise clean and clear surface. The columns separating the three naves were ostentatious and out of scale with the other architectural elements of the church. They seemed to be there for the sole purpose of occupying the space that enclosed them, imposing the glaucous, striated luminosity of their marble. They were the remains of a plundered pagan temple, taking revenge in this church with full force. On the ancient walls, you could see all the sepulchral varieties: medieval, Renaissance, neoclassical, baroque, nineteenth-century, which were more garish, and featured willows and white marble angels crying with their long manes of hair draped over the pedestals. The tomb we were headed to was, again, an alien element in this space. It had a light-gray granite shrine and a portal that could fit a car leading into a black hole. To the side, there was a statue of a hooded monk with his face in the shadows, pointing at the imminent abyss that could swallow us all at any moment. The effect was theatrical and sowed consistent doubts about the joys of resurrection.

While the Australian was taking photos from different angles, I went over to the arch that led to the next chapel so I could observe the whole interior of the church. I became aware of how much pastiche had accumulated over the centuries: an eclectic mix, not the stuff of tourist guides. I leaned against a gate decorated with iron leaves and flowers, then I turned again toward the main nave and stared at the false abyss of the monk's grave.

Suddenly, everything seemed out of balance. This mess of baroque angels, Romanesque arches, Romantic capuchins, and Roman columns made every element even more jarring and disengaged from one another, creating a heterogeneous totality. That's probably how God works. I thought of those ascetic places of worship that tried to create an experience of God's presence through absence—such as the chapel at the clinic or those churches designed by modern architects—and the result was a homogeneity in style, as if they had been created in a single instant and by a single artist. I preferred the Italian-village version: God expressed through an excess of time and creation, chance, dissonance, contradictions. God can't be something as delicate as emptiness, or as simple as the unmistakable. For Him, all matter is useful, even unfulfilled duties, even big noses.

—It's beautiful. We don't have this much art in Australia—said the old man. —Who is buried in the tomb with the monk?

—A famous opera singer from the last century. He was born in this town.

The cemetery, a kilometer outside the village, was disappointing. The tombs only dated back to the end of the eighteenth century. But my new friend didn't seem disappointed. He was photographing several monuments decorated with marble statues and asking me to translate some of the tombstones. It was easier to translate Italian than this "tomb Latin." The inscriptions on plaques tried to express powerful emotions, and usually ended with ellipses or exclamation points. I noticed the influence of fashionable singers on the more recent tombstones, and of opera on the older ones: *Mother: With your angelic smile, you departed, and you left your children in desolation.* Or: *Marcelito: Two days after a day that was full of glory for you, but filled with darkness for us, you left the arms of your mother, whom you loved so much, for the embrace of the Virgin Mary, who loves you so. But we want to tell you that we miss your laughter, your warm caresses, and we forgive all your pranks, even the horrible one where you burned our best hen. We derive com-*

fort from knowing that you are with the Blessed Virgin and that we will meet again soon! The grave had been abandoned for at least fifty years. On every plaque, you found—beneath all the pretense and refinement—authentic love, from sons and daughters, parents, men and women, all intertwined.

After a while, my old Australian began to order me around a bit too much for my liking. As soon as I could, I snuck into the area with the humble tombs. The inscriptions here were shorter, clearer, and didn't fear exaggeration: *We will not forget you, you can count on it! ... You really upset us, man!*

After asking me to translate another tombstone, and taking some notes and photos, the old man said we were missing one thing.

—Are there no tombs from the old days? If the church is so old, how come there are no old tombs in the cemetery?

I asked the florist. The previous cemetery had been transferred because it took up too much space. An orchard now grew in its place, which was famous in the region for its giant beans.

—Imagine—the florist said—people even come from Bologna to buy these beans! Some women say they are miraculous, that they have healing powers. They are delicious. If you want, I can sell you a few kilos ...

—Thanks, but I'm traveling, how would you have me cook them?

—Take them as a token of love. They're also great for love. A young man like yourself, traveling ... it can't be easy. All the women here are decent ... unless someone gives you the address to the only place where ...

She paused and looked at me intently.

—Don't finish. How do you want me to eat the beans in September? It's not even cold yet.

—Ah! But our cannellini beans are famous for travelers. They were used by the pilgrims in the Middle Ages to travel safely to Rome. You must put three hundred and sixty-five beans in a bag with some rosemary. It never fails if you want to reach your destination.

—Listen, I'm not going to Rome. Besides, they also give me indigestion.

—Ah, but ours are famous because they're so easy to digest! They have healing properties for the stomach, for colds, for anemia, for constipation, and baldness, and much more. What is it? You don't eat beans over there?

—Hold on! We have a bean stew that ... not even in your dreams ... It has lots of meat seared in the same oil you sauté the garlic, a beautiful amount of bell peppers, a bit of red chorizo and potatoes. My family had a cook from the mountains that made a stew you would die for. The secret, she used to say, was to get the beans and the potatoes just right, and most important, you had to skip the tomatoes, that's an Italian thing. They also have oxalic acid, which is toxic.

—Your cook said that?

—No. A doctor did.

—To avoid the *pomodoro*?!

—Indeed.

—Savages. If you buy the beans, I'll give you a recipe to prepare them with tomato sauce. That way you'll learn a little about civilization.

—Listen, tomatoes are native to America.

—Oh the lies! Don't make me laugh! The *pomodoro* ... from America?! from South America?!

—Ok fine, tomatoes are from wherever you want … But what happened with the old tombs?

—The merchants and the antique dealers took everything.

—And the bodies?

—To the ossuary—she pointed to a conical building. —There wasn't that much. Everything rots here. Nothing is preserved. If you only knew. The florist's expression changed from a smile to an exaggerated expression of pain.—How my bones hurt sometimes with this arthritis … what a curse!

The woman told me some of the rumors she'd heard in her many years working the entrance of the cemetery. I translated the stories to the Australian couple, and added a few details of my own.

—The bones from the old cemetery were reserved for building a chapel—I explained to them brazenly.

—What do you mean?

—Yes, here in Italy, when a cemetery is too large, you simply can't let it compete with farmland. Italy isn't Australia. Here, they recycle the best parts. It's always been like that. Etruscan sarcophagi are reoccupied by Roman tenants, Gothic stelae are sanded off and reinscribed, fervent Catholics await resurrection under the watch of pagan gods. It's a form of ecumenism: tolerance to save money for funerals. They'll stab each other over the sex of the angels, but when it comes to paying for the funeral, they forget their differences. Sometimes you'll find cadavers from different centuries sharing the same grave. But an even better solution is to build the chapels with the bones themselves. If you go to Rome, you should visit the Capuchin Crypt in Via Veneto. It's all human bones. Lamps are made out of sacrums: sacred light emanates from what used to be someone's genitals (a magnificent idea, if you ask me, imagine staring at the stars through someone's beautiful asshole). The angels on the altars are actually the tiny skeletons of the little Barberini princes who died during the plague. As they say in Rome: *quod non fecit barbari, fecit Barberini*; "what the barbarians didn't do, the Barberini did."

—Are you making fun of us? —asked Sarah incredulously.

—No. Go look for yourselves. There's another crypt in Milan, but it is very tall and not too stable; they had to use wire to keep all the femurs and skulls in place to prevent a collapse ... Without all these chapels, *all* of Europe would be a cemetery. This continent has more dead than square meters ... Take the archaeologists for instance: they take small cameras for their field work, and sonar devices to look for ancient tombs. When they find one, several meters under an olive grove or cornfield, they drill a tiny hole, and use their special cameras to take photos. If they find valuable objects, they open the whole thing up; if they don't, guess what?! they leave it for the peasants to continue plowing on top of it. People don't like graveyards to get too big at the expense of seeds. Better to plant beans ... like they've done here.

—This whole thing about digging out cemeteries sounds sacrilegious to me; completely disrespectful —the old man remarked, while taking more photos. —How do you know so much about tombs?

—It's in my family. My father built a giant catacomb on his land, two hundred feet tall and made out of black marble. That's where he buried his first wife, who was only twenty-three years old, with all her jewelry. He liked Edgar Allan Poe.

The Australians looked at each other.

—A tomb two hundred feet tall! —said Charles. You must be joking. You've been mocking us this entire time!

But the old man wasn't upset; in fact, he seemed quite pleased.

—Well, yes ... I was joking, but now I'll tell you the truth: in my country, there are natives who not only shrink their dead enemies' heads, but also their entire bodies. They basically turn them into dolls, barely a half-foot tall. And their women consider them the most precious of ornaments; they wouldn't trade them for anything, not even diamonds. No one knows the purpose of this shrinking process.

—Oh yes, I did hear something about this. I think it's very interesting —said Charles— but it's not a good idea. Those savages, why don't they bury their enemies?

When the old man realized that my travel plans were somewhat flexible, he invited me to ride with them in their car, an American model, three times longer than the little Fiats people used around here. It was a convertible with two doors, four headlights, and a vertical bar that passed through what must have been the middle of the radiator. When I got in, I noticed the huge metal cradle was much more balanced than in the taxis in Milan. I made myself comfortable in the back seat.

—Do you like my Firebird? —asked Charles.

—It must make better time than the trains here.

—It's a great car, for real men. It's the most precious thing I own ... after my Sarah, of course.

I couldn't reconcile Charles's taste for art with his taste for juvenile sports cars.

—Yes, a car for men, but not for the Irish. The original name was Banshee; Pontiac had already distributed the publicity brochures and taken down payments for the first models, when someone at the factory—some know-it-all—pointed out that a *banshee* was a supernatural being in Irish folklore, a woman who wails about her family's death. So, of course, they had to change the name to Firebird. Oddly, many customers, who had already made the down payment, decided to take their money back; offended Irishmen, I suppose. In the United States, of course, they were talking about anti-Irish discrimination. I come from a Polish family and I couldn't care less about these things. I like the car because of its technical features: it performs much better than a Camaro or Mustang. Would you like to take it for a drive?

—I don't know how to drive.

—How is that possible? —shouted Sarah, sounding extremely worried, as if I had announced I had leprosy. —We'll have to do something about that.

We stopped to explore both the abandoned churches that appeared along the way. We were traveling on local roads, and it was a cumbersome process, but my companions seemed to enjoy it. You had to ask around for the local who kept the key to the church, then when you finally did find him, you had to tip him to get in.

As I walked around the dark and empty spaces, my companions studied every stone, calling me every now and then to translate some inscription. They were very impressed with my pretend Latin, based on the roots of the words, the brevity of the epitaphs, the obvious significance of the tombstone, the impossibility that the dead would correct me, and, above all, whatever came to my head.

My new friends looked at my coat and then my eyes.

—How do you know all these things, Mario?

I shrugged and pretended to be modest.

* * *

The sun was already setting when we left the second church.

—It's late—said Sarah. —Why don't you have dinner with us, and then we'll take you to the train station so you can go back to your hotel?

—I don't have a hotel.

My friends stared at each other.

—Well, we've taken you out of your way, why don't you stay with us? —Charles said. —I'll pay for you; you'll be my guest.

I accepted, and imagined finally showering. We arrived at a five-star hotel that was partly built into some old abbey wall. This explained why it was called *Albergue de la Vieja Abadía*. The employees could barely hide their surprise when they saw me, but respectfully followed the old man's orders. Using two fingers, a guy in buttons carried my little bag to the room. When I tried to give him the few lira I had left, he smiled and winked at me. —There's no need— he said.

I found myself in a room with an infinite bed and its own bathroom. I showered for half an hour, the water washing away soil from every hamlet in Italy. I put on my only pair of pants and the same coat, but changed my shirt. From the window, I could see a stone village on a hill with a steeple standing out. I was sure my friends had visited it already. In the distance, a train crossed the plain, headed toward some cement buildings at the foot of the hill, the "modern" neighborhood of the village.

Scattered on the plain were rows of cypresses and poplars: vertical lines holding the earth at ninety-degree angles. I remembered the pampas of my childhood where there were no trees, no hills, no hotels, just an endless expanse, a floating land that defeated even the best of painters. I come from a land that escapes one's grasp, made of materials that turn into dreams and doubts the moment you turn your back; it's an aerial place, where categories make no sense.

My new friends were waiting for me at the bar and were on time. We drank a few whiskeys, then moved over to the dining room. The waiters treated this old couple with the utmost respect, and me with a certain camaraderie. For them, it was very important to make clear they understood the social differences, but their tone with me began to change when I ordered a bottle of Barolo. Sarah hesitated before ordering a burger; the old man asked the maître d':

—I suppose that during summer you don't do bean dishes, right?

—But of course, *signore*. We currently have a bean carpaccio.

He sounded like a Hollywood actor playing an Italian speaking English.

—What is carpaccio?

—It's meat cut into very thin strips, like sheets of paper, and served raw with cooked beans. The secret—he said, turning to Sarah—is a little bit of rosemary, virgin olive oil, and, of course, cannellini beans from Molcone, a village close to here. They say their beans bring good luck for business. You must make a good meal with the famous cannellini, eat them, and fart three times; then a business is guaranteed to be prosperous and the partners won't fight with each other.

—Very well, bring me the carpaccio.

—I recommend you accompany it with a good red wine from Fiesole, *signore*.

—No, I'll have what Mario is having.

—Tell me —I asked the maître d'— does the carpaccio have tomatoes?

—No, no tomatoes. The base is *capuchina* lettuce, with a bit of raw onion passed through hot water.

—Then, I'll have one too.

When the carpaccio arrived, Sarah was amazed at how thin they'd managed to cut the raw meat, but she didn't want to try it.

—How do you achieve this? —she asked the maître d'.

—Only for you, *signora*, the secret is to put the meat in the freezer for ten minutes before you slice it.

The food was outstanding and simple: the hearty dishes held up to the wine, the flavors were fresh like the soft breezes entering the windows and bringing a bit of autumn with them. Charles ate ceremoniously: he took a small bite of raw meat, almost transparent, with two or three beans, and chewed slowly with his eyes closed.

—Hmm! Tastes great.

—Those beans once fed all of Europe —I said.

Sometimes, during the meal, I felt guilty about paying more attention to the wine than to my generous hosts. I asked for another bottle. The more we ate, they more affectionate they became. They told me about their travels through Italy: no fixed itinerary, they were free, and—needless to say—they had plenty of money. I tried to estimate how many bottles of wine they were willing to pay for. Their questions made me think they overestimated me; like Eligia, they assumed that all knowledge is hard-earned. We talked about my country, and I was struck by how much I was just making up. Lying made me feel more secure; the strangeness of everything allowed me to do so with pure, fanciful pleasure.

They tried to get me to talk about my life; but I don't open up to anyone. I don't tell anything about my life that can be dangerous; I prefer to lie. My defense strategy was to turn their questions back on them.

—I only have a few siblings back home, that's all—the old man seemed embarrassed. —We lost our only son. I guess I blame those damn Firebirds … It must have been something with the brakes, though the people from the insurance company didn't want to acknowledge it. My Andrew was the best driver in Canberra and for many miles around. He was a great man … We should've had more children, but my youth was difficult, and I married late. I would have liked to study medicine, but we worked a lot, you know? And then, that terrible car accident … No, you wouldn't know what it's like to lose a child, what it's like to bury him. I did it all with my own hands, the entire service. It had been a while since I'd dug a grave, but I had to do it.

—You're a gravedigger!

—Yes, my entire life. Now I own the company. We're doing well, and with this trip I'm getting ideas for new models, ways of customizing our services. Customs are changing in Australia. There's a high demand for more imagery on the tombs. The less they understand death, the more imagery they need.

—I don't understand death. I *need* those images, you know? Do you understand death?

He refrained from answering.

—We could use a young man like you back there, Mario. Sarah doesn't want to work anymore, not after what happened with Andrew. I have employees, but no one with class, who could stand in the middle of a room, address a heartbroken family, and speak knowledgeably about the different kinds of tombstones we offer while citing in Latin all the popes and kings who chose them. Look, you're even dressed in black already! You wouldn't have to dig the graves yourself, of course. We have people for that, but I won't lie to you, it is hard work to be an ... *undertaker*. That word, Mario, is pretty clear, it's a word that calls to mind hell rather than heaven.

—You think you get used to it professionally—said Sarah—but then one of your own dies and all that is useless. Only God can help you.

—Perhaps Sarah is right—the old man said. —I don't know much about different religions, but ascribing to a single religion wouldn't be good business. I'm in this career because I had to start earning a living at a very young age. What I do know is that I take them six feet under, and that's where I leave them.

From that point on, the roles were reversed. I was the one who led the conversation, making up more stories about Italy or my country, while my friends grew quieter. Ordering the last two bottles of wine was Charles's idea.

The waiters removed all the dishes and glasses, giving me a knowing smile. We'd been there for a while. Then the old man bid me good night, saying —We'll see you in the morning. Do consider our offer. It's a good one.

I didn't need to turn on the lights when I got to the room; a nocturnal glow flooded in through the window. One of the empty drawers was half-open, revealing a fleshy darkness. Unlike the opera singer's tomb, this darkness seemed to hold something it wanted to give back, something unsolicited.

I decided to go for a walk. In the hotel lobby, I saw one of the waiters. He put a few bills in my chest pocket and mumbled something about "commission for the bottles. For Bacchus! What a liver!"

I headed to town. On my way down the hill, I spotted some familiar greenery, the kind I saw in that garden in Milan; but these grew apart and in all directions, as if the restraint they'd shown in spring had given way to the wild and anarchic freedom of summer. On this hillside, the relations articulated in the city garden were subject to a greater totality, not dependent on each element or the relationships between them.

I stared at the complexity in all this darkness. Shadows fused everything, only to multiply into even more shadows and sparks of stolen light from the sky, which the penumbras received as a prized potion: to create, in the night, a collective sense of form.

I thought about the drive in the Firebird—too fast, too many impressions; I couldn't surmise anything from that vertigo. As I walked, the heathers and junipers moved with indifference. I'd been locked up for so many months. The clinic here, the clinic back there, Aron's apartment. These days of aimless wandering had been limited to small villages and train compartments. After three years, it was as if I were taking my first steps outside. There were no longer arches and columns. The aesthetic appreciation that Mr. Bormann instilled in me and I accepted with such pride was now receding into incomprehensible spaces. This night was teaching me its lesson, simplifying everything to its most basic form—transcending individual details to bring coherence to a composition.

The lighter shadows outlined the few trees on the road, their branches swaying softly in the breeze. This wasn't back country. Modern buildings were at the foot of the hill, and the hotel lights behind me grew dimmer with each step. It wasn't a landscape that excluded humanity, it just gently subordinated it.

I remembered how the walls of that building in Milan enclosed the small garden with indifference. The small patch of green was held prisoner, so it invited you to stay in; this hillside, on the other hand, with all its different perspectives, invited you to wander. I considered, for instance, a return to my country, where a beautiful woman no longer waited for me but did love me, and where my home was Aron's cursed apartment. I immediately realized there was no point trying to convince Eligia of an earlier return. There was so little waiting for us. I imagined she'd thought about it many times, and for many more reasons than I did. Another option was for me to go to Geneva, but that would be an intrusion to Eligia's freedom and her right to be bored with Piaget. It was also a request for help I couldn't bring myself to make. The possibility of returning to Milan also occurred to me: to stay at a cheap hotel on credit . . . to look for Dina and ask for help. But asking Dina for assistance would be absurd. After considering all the alternatives, I finally understood I was in no condition to enjoy the freedom offered by this hill.

The fresh breeze and the warmth of the wine produced a stimulating sensation, but what suddenly awakened me was the fear of not wanting to be alone anymore. I regretted babbling so much with the old couple. I picked up the pace; I was no longer wandering. I was running away, and, before I knew it, I was already at the train station.

—When is the next train?

—Going where?
—Anywhere.

The train was packed with students. The compartments and corridors were full; some passengers were sitting or lying on the floor, so tired, they didn't mind leaning on each other. I sat in a corner. I had left my bag in the hotel and wouldn't be able to change clothes for many days. When we arrived at the next station, I got up to go buy a flask of something, but before I could take the first step, the corridor filled up with even more students looking for places to sit. Without a word, they went to sleep, as they were probably doing on the platform. It seemed unfair to wake them up. It must have been Monday: we were probably en route to some college town.

Someone broke the calm silence and shouted: —When are we getting to Bologna?! We should already be there! Another voice, more firm, answered: —There are people in this country who are never satisfied! You give them a train, and now they want schedules as well!

I felt outraged by the offer from my Australian friends. One shouldn't go around asking strangers to take over their business. Besides, I couldn't accept their job. I didn't even speak Latin, it would be dishonest. In retrospect, I heard Charles's paternal tone and seemed to recall some motherly gestures from Sarah. This made me even more uncomfortable. I could wander around a few more days and return to Milan. I would like to chat with some of these students, my travel companions, and share with them what I saw on the hillside, but these days no one talks about Nature. I would sound ridiculous.

After twenty minutes of the train rattling, a young soprano voice, unexpected in the dark, asked her companion:

—Did you read the Party report?

—Yes, I did.

—What are they saying this time?

—That the working class is more impoverished than ever. This exploitation can no longer be tolerated: the workers are wearing berets because they don't even have money to buy a simple cap.

—I wear a beret because that's what the Cubans do.

—They say the working class consumes less meat than in the last century, that capitalist complacency is causing Party members to stay home watching television, instead of attending meetings.

—Did I tell you my family bought a TV? Do you have one?

—We've had one for three years. Now my dad is even considering getting a Fiat 600. Grandfather can't believe it. He says we're betraying the cause... Did you see the live broadcast from San Remo? I like the new Celentano. He's no longer acting like a clown. Hey, are you sure this is the express train to Bologna?

—No ... —interrupted a young male voice—this one stops at Rimini. It's a local train.

—No, no—assured a fourth voice, indefinable in the dark—this is a special train to Padua, it's unlisted. But it won't stop in Bologna.

—But does anyone know when we'll arrive?

IX

... I feel thee ere I see thy face;
Look up, and let me see our doom in it.

—J. Keats (*Hyperion*, I, 96–97)

I RETURNED TO MILAN two days after the date we had agreed on; Eligia had already settled back in the room. She was lively; the break had reenergized her, and she was ready to resume the treatment. The most uneven areas of her face had disappeared thanks to the "matter" provided by the second flap, and she could feel new possibilities in her flesh. The doctors didn't make her wait; in the first surgery of this stage she came out of the operating room with a great novelty: eyelids. I thought they did an acceptable job. Though she couldn't close her eyes all the way, it was enough to make the nights less eerie ... now the naked eyeballs were basically covered.

With the new substance, her face began to reappear, or at

least her general outline. With a certain disdain in her smile, the maid with the spicy breath said:

—You wanted *biombos*? Well, here they are.

And she pointed to Eligia's flaring eyelids.

I didn't see Dina in my daily excursions to the bar. I asked about her, but the bartender did not know much.

—She's been gone for two months. Word on the street is that she got married.

Ten days after the eyelid surgery, Eligia's vision began to get blurry, and her right eye was tearing up. The doctors examined her carefully. They looked uncomfortable when they returned from the treatment room. Professor Calcaterra addressed me with a solemn tone.

—My chief assistant, Dr. Risso, who oversaw the last surgery, has something to explain.

Professor Calcaterra was very cold toward his colleague. The chief assistant led me to a corner and spoke in a low voice.

—Mr. Mario, there is a small inconvenience. Due to an oversight for which I'm entirely responsible, the arm skin that we used to reconstruct the right eyelid was applied incorrectly.

—I don't think it looks that bad.

—We used skin from the arm, and the epidermis was put facing in, instead of out.

—Is that bad?

—It wouldn't be bad at all, except that we didn't notice there were active follicles, so now small hairs are growing under the eyelid and, of course, they are very irritating to the eye.

—So you need to reconstruct the whole eyelid again?

—We've discussed this with your mother, and she agreed

that it would be best to leave it like this for now. Later on, we'll see. We could use electricity, but that's a long treatment. That would have to be done when you return to your country. And if the electric hair removal doesn't work, then yes, it would have to be reconstructed; but for now, all we have to do is turn the eyelid over every ten or fifteen days and use a pair of tweezers to remove the hairs.

When Professor Calcaterra saw the stunned expression on my face, he approached me and led me to the bed.

—Look—he pointed with his usual frankness at the scars. —It's the end of the chaos. Yes, there are some marks and some inconveniences, as my assistant explained, but these are scars of order, of reason. The attack that unleashed chaos in the flesh has been exorcised by these scars, which now serve as the boundaries between the past and future, between hate and faith, a faith that will have to lean on these marks. I'll confess a secret: I've seen so many severe scars ... that at this point in my life, I believe a body creates to overcome the designs of the human form—it surpasses itself, when it surpasses nature. He glanced at Eligia, whose face, re-created by science, showed incomprehension. —Don't let prejudice get the best of you—he added, turning to her. —"Abnormal" is a word that the impotent throw enviously at creation from their sad, normal lives.

For the rest of our stay in Milan, and even after our return, my life and my drinking revolved around Eligia's eyelid. The day of the epilation, I would drink just enough to have a steady hand. Eligia had thirty years of experience from her marriage to Aron detecting even the smallest trace of alcohol; my precautions were such that they bordered on recovery. When the crucial moment arrived, I would ask her if it would perhaps be best to call a nurse, but she preferred I did it. I never dared to find out how much she understood this situation. Years later, I still wondered whether she had asked me to do the epilation—putting her own eye at risk—in order to control my alcoholism. The thought of it was enough for me, and it probably saved my life.

By the third or fourth session, I was getting quite good at the task. The key was to support my wrist on a small pillow and use a magnifying glass. In the augmented image of the eye, I could see the detail of every vessel, the palpitating reverse of the skin, the trembling orb. I was very thorough, even at the risk of pulling too much, because I wanted to ensure she wouldn't feel any discomfort in the eye for the next ten days.

This gave me almost a full week to drink.

Our second autumn in Milan went by between hair-plucking sessions and reading. Eligia was more attentive, and I had to repeat fewer chapters as she was also more engaged, which allowed us to discuss what we read.

Mentions of skin from the outside world no longer sounded so sarcastic: ads about beauty products, for instance, had lost their sense of derision. Eligia even sent me to buy some makeup so she could try to even the tones between the original skin and the grafts.

In November, Eligia sent me on an errand that had nothing to do with her treatment.

—Mario, it would be great if you could go to the university's administration. It's not very far from here. In their archives, they might still have the papers from a conference that I gave in '46. I was so young, and Aron was dressed so sharp! He had a tailor make him an overcoat with a fur lining and collar for the European winter. When he entered the auditorium, I heard a man ask if he was the Russian ambassador. Him and his black coat! It was the autumn of 1946, November, I'm fairly certain—before we moved to Switzerland. Do you remember? You were so little. You were scared of the rubble because you thought there were Egyptian mummies hiding in it, like the ones we had seen at the museums. Who could have given you those ideas?... Milan was still in shambles from the bombardments. The city is unrecognizable today. They told me back then that they had begun reconstructing *before* the end of the war, and then after it was bombed again, they kept on rebuilding. How they worked! If you only remembered. The Piazza San Fedele, the San Babila area, the Royal Palace. You saw the façades intact, but behind was all rubble and ruins about to collapse. What struck me the most was seeing the sky through the windows instead of the interior of a building ... I remember a caryatid: her head and breasts in a single white block among the debris piled up behind a façade. She could have been one of the famous caryatids from the Royal Palace... The nonsense that stays with us... Based on her weapons, she looked like an Athena, but her head didn't have a helmet.

I asked the doctors for directions to the university. —Ah! *La Ca'Grande*—exclaimed one of the professor's assistants, and he gave me some directions to walk there.

The façade of the building featured too many ornamental motifs: terra-cotta busts of prophets and sages mounted on prominent medallions above the twin windows. The characters were placed in awkward positions, some with their arms extending out, gesticulating and admonishing. To me they looked like creatures digging themselves out of the wall and trying to escape that prison. I feared one of those busts might succeed and plunge into the street. I wondered what those sages and prophets would do once they were free.

The clerk had no trouble finding the presentations of Eligia's conference in the archives. —There is no problem from '46 on; the problem is '45 and back. This building was bombed, but the archives were rescued faster than some humans. It contains a thousand years of history!

The conference was about "Boarding Schools in Prominent Nations." It took me two hours to make copies, two hours of old and boring statistics. When I said goodbye, the clerk suggested I take a tour of the building. —I recommend the *quadreria*—he said.

In the distant past, this building had been the city's main hospital. Portraits of its benefactors who had supported *Ca'Grande* were on display. They were excellent portraits. As I was about to leave, an old man in a guard's uniform came over.

—Did you enjoy it? *Bello*, eh? All these good lords, so generous, who donated their fortunes to help the sick. Great examples! The hospital commissioned the portraits in recognition of their gifts: a half body meant it was a large donation; a full body meant it was exceptional; an equestrian portrait meant they gave their fortune. The bigger the donation, the larger and more magnificent the portrait. It's only fair. They would be displayed on the porticos every odd year, on March 25, for the Annunciation of the Blessed Virgin.

He came closer and whispered:

—Not all the portraits are of the highest quality, though.

The painters expected a good tip from the rich donors, especially those who deserved the equestrian portrait. But if the tip didn't live up to the artist's expectations—he looked at me menacingly from his small stature—the portrait wouldn't be a perfect work of art. The horses suffered the most. If the donor protested, the artist responded that the gentleman's generosity with the hospital was indisputable, but the same thing couldn't be said about the horse. The guard drew the palm of his hand up to my navel. —But if we consider this carefully, the donors were actually lucky. It's not often that our image in posterity depends on what tips we can provide.

A thick fog descended over the street, a gray luminosity that absorbed the buildings and trees, penetrating them until nothing was left; it was a veil that enveloped lines and volumes, leaving only a trace of what had been. On my way back to the clinic, I walked along an endless fence of golden spears protecting the gardens of a public building. Once again, the first great fog of the year had taken me by surprise in the street. The gray that devoured the world so calmly began to take on a bluish tone, a translucent vapor with celestial droplets that dissolved in the still and unassailable mist, just when they seemed to be within hand's reach. I focused on the vanishing perspective of golden spears. Time and memory followed the fading forms. Only the golden glow survived as it fled toward the vanishing point. Little by little, the fog began to incorporate the golden light of the points. It seemed as if the gold tones and the translucency had entered a vacillating fate. When the mist had finally swallowed the fence, I would be completely lost. Fortunately, the gold began to slowly regain its strength and reassert itself. And it was then, as the fog dissipated from the golden touch on its bosom, that the thread of my thoughts suddenly returned, and with it, the memory of Dina.

The next day I began reading the old conference paper to Eligia. Ten minutes in, I noticed she was asleep. I stopped, and she woke up a few minutes later.

—I was so young ... This was my conference ... but the schools were built by the General and his wife. What nonsense. Just throw it away.

At last, the doctors announced the date when we would be able to return to our country. March of 1967, they said. I didn't feel particularly happy, but Eligia was encouraged by the news. Twenty months had passed, and she couldn't wait to see her other children.

Thirty days before our return, I went back to the old corner bar. Someone pulled gently on the sleeve of my coat. It was Dina. She had gained some weight and was wearing a big apron.

—What are you doing here?

—I was looking for you.

—Where have you been all this time?

—Did you miss me? I'm working for a dog groomer. I started sweeping the dog hair, but I quickly moved up to grooming. A friend and I plan to open a hair salon in our district.

—For people?

—For dogs. And I also bought a Fiat 600 on credit!

For the first time, she invited me to her home. Based on how her neighbors treated her, I deduced she had moved recently.

She started picking me up in her 600 every afternoon from that day forward, and I didn't say anything about her changes. She went out of her way to make me happy, preparing some kind of surprise every day.

She introduced me to her aunt, who lived with her and was almost seventy. The first thing the aunt said when Dina left us alone was: —What is happening to her? Is she really in love with you? You're very important to her ... and to me. But Dina, who came back to the living room, told her to shush, pretending to be upset.

I was able to spend a lot of time with Dina, now that Eligia did not need as much help. At night, the aunt retired to her room early and we would stay in the living room, kissing and watching television shows that rivaled the ones from my country in their stupidity.

Dina sensed the shortcomings of her ambition, but clung to it with great intensity. She acted with confident hope. She didn't ask me to change my shirt or stop drinking; she didn't give me new ties or a new coat. She hadn't suddenly become some Italian miracle. And I was grateful for that. She did make me take my pants or shirt off when she noticed a loose button, and would sew it back herself. I let her do this without asking. There was a certain vulnerability in her, a tacit willingness to be humiliated, which made me fear for her future, and what the economic miracle would do to her. It never occurred to me I would be part of that future.

Every night, when it was time to go, she would prepare me a cup of *Canarino* and walk me to the front door of the building. There she would press against me and kiss me with excessive force.

* * *

The night before my departure, with the plane ticket already in my pocket, I hadn't told her I was about to leave. Still, she maintained her affectionate openness, which showed in her modest apartment, where she imbued everything with a sense of anticipation, as if something new, something promising were about to happen. The furniture was incredibly shabby, but she had added plants in every corner, which grew and flowered.

That night, Dina had another one of her surprises in store for me. Before going to the apartment, we stopped at a butcher shop—a place with marble, and display cases showing the meat on beautifully arranged leaves of lettuce. She asked for two steaks costing three hundred and fifty lire *l'etto*: one was two hundred grams and another, half a kilo.

—I want to make you a good South American meal to invigorate you!

Back at the apartment, her aunt took care of the cooking. —Juicy and rare—recommended Dina, looking at me as if she knew all my tastes. Then she went to take a bath, and I stayed with the old woman in the kitchen.

—Would you like a little wine? —she asked.

She poured me a glass without waiting for a response. The aunt had some soda. We stood in silence for a few minutes as the meat began to sizzle on the skillet, then the old woman started to prepare a few other things. The room smelled of spices.

—So you like meat raw and without seasoning? I like risotto. The first spice you use in risotto is gersal; then you add other spices, but

if the base with the gersal isn't prepared right, you can say goodbye to the risotto! My sister used to prepare wonderful knishes with just a little bit of onion; and she made the best falafel, she seasoned the garbanzo beans very well and mashed them. It had so much flavor, you thought you were eating white meat!... Before the war, everything tasted good. Your mouth watered just thinking about the food we had. There were spices that helped us fight the cold, cereals offered in this land, recipes of our grandmothers, which they used their entire lives ... But then came the war ... What a curse! Everything changed, one day in 1943. That was before the bombs. I was carrying Dina in my arms to take her back home, then I saw a car with those men stopped in front of the building where Dina lived with her mother, father, and brothers. I lowered my head and decided to go to my building instead, which was right next to theirs, and I closed all the windows. Thank God my Dinita was so young she couldn't understand what was happening!... They took her mother to the north for helping the partisans. We went to stay in Padana since we had friends there with a farm. It wasn't easy to find a safe place ... In those years, not everyone wanted to be associated with me, you know. These people in Padana were old friends and they had bought the farm in 1919, when we thought the Bolsheviks were coming ... But in 1944, as the situation kept getting worse, they got scared and asked us to leave. I didn't even know how I was going to get back to Milan. On the way back, we were lucky, and a truck with four Blackshirts picked us up. I remember seeing a poster in the cabin that said "Make good, or get out." When we returned to Milan, everything had gotten worse. Poor city! It's the one that suffered the longest: from the time that this whole dark history started, just after the peace, from 1918, to the last day, when they hung Mussolini here with that poor girl who didn't understand anything ... In Milan, the shops had no merchandise. Those from the government said it was to prevent looting during the air-raid alarms, but the truth is the merchants didn't have anything to sell. There was also nothing to eat. Dina and I had nowhere to go. We went to see my sister's apartment, and you could still smell the food. My sister had been the queen of the kitchen, serving real food, not meat on a plate! But we were afraid of staying there or in the apartment where I used to live, so we found a few rooms in an abandoned building. I made a little money cleaning and cooking for some German officers. Their food at the barracks was disgusting. The men, they said, did the cooking, and the stews were just inedible—always overcooked—and there were sausages instead of fresh meat. Burnt oil kept on being used, potatoes came apart when you touched them with a fork, and the beans were hard as bones. They would send me to the black market to buy good ingredients and cook them a decent meal. I always put a little bit aside for my little girl, who had to stay by herself while I was away. In the afternoon, when I went to the apartment where they ate and did other things, it was already dark. Imagine walking outside in the winter, in the dark, with all the fog, and during the curfew. The streets outside the center of the city were like holes. I was afraid of these streets; it was not a good time to be walking around. But before I could even start cooking, I had to cross half the city just to get a little bit of salt. There was a state monopoly, and the salt mines were controlled by the Allies. In the black market, salt was almost as expensive as the medicine coming from Switzerland. Imagine, no salt! And I like to prepare my risotto with gersal. *You need lots of coarse salt for risotto; you have to put it at the bottom of the pot and toast it with sesame, and you have to pay attention to the sesame because if it toasts too much, it'll be bitter ... Ah, yes, my dear! In those days everything was soaked in a bitter rage, cold like the fog of these streets.*

—I know that fog very well.

—*This was not normal anger. My people knew the kind where there is always a place for reconciliation. You can be angry and still head toward reconciliation. Anger can touch others, unite them, and they surpass it. But anger can separate from reconciliation, and then it becomes pure hate—cold and isolating. In those times, anger was tough to reckon with, it didn't care about anything. The truth is no one knew what to do with it; it was clear that those who possessed it wanted everyone to see their power. They had no shame ... Those were years when laws became a thing of the distant past, they no longer meant anything. And what we had, you could barely call norms. I grew up with rules and severe punishments, but at least there were rules. Our laws had history; they taught us how to live together. You could engage with those laws and they answered back; you could talk to people about them. I think madness takes over when you realize laws have been made against love, against others' existence, and they are created not to reward good behavior, but to achieve a complete coldness. Those cold laws fell on us ... What I had to endure during those winters!... You already drank another glass?*

—It's good.

—*... our old laws might have been "laws like fire," but at least it was the fire of the home.*

—There's no better place than home.

The old woman removed the steaks from the plate; they were past ready.

—*He lived in those laws, who speaks close to you without showing His face. Why should we be able to see it when we can't even see our own? The face receives everything—the eyes, the ears, the mouth, even the cheeks, which can receive blows. The face was meant for us to know the depths of each other. That's why it is so sacred ...*

—Yes, the face is sacred.

— *... because it's already the Other. People should think of the face as the cradle of love. A true face is one where there is a will to love; without love, the face is just meat, something horrific. The whole world has forgotten about fear. Before, fear could change a face. Now, I look around and realize that I'm the only one who is afraid. When you're afraid, nature, the taste of food, even fear itself changes ... I became afraid the day they took Dina's mother. Just going out on the street was a feat. I imagined my route step-by-step, and all the places where someone in a uniform would stop me. From that day on, I felt detached from everything. I couldn't even stay locked in that abandoned apartment, because I knew it wasn't my home. I would listen to the still silence in the stairway; my footsteps were the only sound filling up the space. I felt as if a force from outside were pressing against the walls and about to open the latch. It was maddening, sitting still all the time, looking at that doorknob. I imagined someone standing on the other side, lurking in silence. Everyone had the right to condemn someone to death. The person that smiled one day could be the same one accusing you the next. How the faces of those bastards changed! It seemed incredible that they were the same people. One man, two faces. Nowadays, everything is different. With peace, faces remain the same. But I know that it's enough for some politician to start saying idiocies, and those faces begin to split again. Don't you agree?*

—No! Of course, I agree.

—*What kind of face could a person who is beyond guilt, who lives in the bureaucracy of evil, truly have? "One doesn't know beforehand the face of His messenger," as our doctor's grandmother used to say. At least, if I may add, we know that in the chosen moment, the face won't be revealed under helmets or visor caps, or behind black glasses! The fascists used all of those so we could only see their lips, their indifferent mouths. The face only reveals itself in love. One had to see those empty homes after they came and took all the people by force.*

—What a horror! I consider myself an enemy of violence, you know?

—It was obvious those homes wouldn't see a reunion, no memory remained of the lives people had shared there. No mother would cook again in one of those kitchens . . .

Dina interrupted the old woman's monologue. Without saying a word, the aunt went to her room. We ate the dry meat in the living room, silent and happy, under the watchful eye of a Paul Newman poster. After the meal, I had a few whiskeys, thinking that, were it not for my flight the next day, this would be a good opportunity to bring things to a close: a few kisses, two words . . . and Dina would completely forget about the nocturnal and evanescent apparition of the past twenty months. I was certain that she would have no trouble becoming a faithful companion, be it by indolence or sympathy. But I confess that what attracted me most to her was precisely that nocturnal evanescence that freed me from all compromise. Back then, I thought that I had kept my part of the bargain: I had never asked her for help.

She kissed me and undressed. Her arms and legs were long. The volumes of her compact body revealed themselves timidly, creating soft but firm shadows. Everything in her was positive matter that didn't need to support any abysses. Her skin awaited touch, and the possibility of this caress produced in me an anticipation similar to what I felt when lowering my hand on a polished statue with my eyes closed. Except Dina's body wasn't marble or any other rock; it almost surprised me when I touched it and it yielded where my finger had pressed the upper end of her sternum.

In the living room, on the furniture's cold and brightly colored plastic, Dina's body stood out by contrast. It was her willingness to accept everything, and the confidence that she could take it all. I looked at her closely: her face asserted its presence, so delicate and remarkable, and at the same time, it achieved a perfect balance with her naked body. With a turn of the head, like the shot of an arrow, her neck tendon transported my gaze from the triangle of her eyes and mouth to that of her nipples and navel. My eyes leapt from her face to her body, and from her body to her face ... Artists are victims of their styles—I thought—no painter had achieved this equilibrium between a portrait and a nude.

My eyes paused on her face. The arch of her forehead and eyebrows coincided near the center, but separated slightly at the temples revealing the outline of a bone underneath the thin skin. Her eyelids didn't need makeup: the bony orbits bent the light around her sunken eyes, creating a natural shadow.

Dina was a woman who liked to lean on her elbows as soon as she got a chance. Many times I had seen her leaning on the counter at the bar or on the ledge of the wall at Corso, while talking to a client. When she did this, her shoulders would rise almost to the level of her cheeks, and you began to appreciate the uniqueness of her body, so different from those of the neorealist divas in vogue during those years of abundance. You had to have courage to work with that body back then. She walked with a helpless, quixotic air, but, fortunately, there was little competition in that quiet sector away from the city center.

One day, at the bar, shortly after we met, she struck one of those elbow poses—this time on top of the jukebox as it played "The Boy from Gluck Street" by a dull Calentano—I observed her arm first, then a fragment of it until I was so focused, her skin was a plane without reference. That is how I learned to appreciate the pristine nature of that skin, pale and predisposed to be revived, with a hypnotic quality that invited the observer to clear the mind. From that day forward, I got used to observing fragments of her, abstractions of her body. But this night at her apartment, after eating the succulent steak that was reinvigorating and also dry, I observed her body in its totality for the first time.

I realized with alarm that I was the only witness to that moment. The impression of Dina's body, which had already pierced my eyes and seeped into my memory, had transformed into a responsibility, a pact that, without words or any signatures, would bind me for life to that image. I imagined something similar must hide behind all commitment: images that make us sole witnesses and keepers of that which is most precious and fragile in a person, their contingent existence, which needs our testimony not to disappear. It is an obligation to live and hold on to the best moments of the being we love. I felt uncomfortable.

* * *

Dina stood and finished undressing. She looked thin, almost without volume, but as she leaned back on the sofa, curves of unforeseen sensuality began to rise, and the triangle of her navel and nipples teased like a taut sail, with defined muscles in the abdomen, and elongated lines along the arms. In each movement, in each torsion, a new Venus appeared briefly, one moment with the calf pressed against the thigh, then with the abdomen contracting as the knees raised. Small folds of skin and fat appeared unsuspected as the body moved.

As she lay on the fabric—green and yellowing, rigid and artificial—her powerful hips emerged from her previously thin frame. I wondered how bone and skin could bend with so much flexibility. The pelvis had become the dominant stroke that unleashed the other forms of the body. Her thigh gained coherence in its proximity to the hip, echoing a rhythm that announced or resolved the powerful pull of the sacroiliac joint; in whatever direction the gaze took, every form in Dina's body invited comprehension of the next. I saw that beauty is totality, a continuity that develops in all its possibilities.

Leaning back on the couch, Dina propped herself on one elbow while her free arm rested over her waist and her hand was on the upholstery. I wanted to preserve that instant too. The two steps that separated us produced a Dina that was complete and new. We were left suspended for a few seconds.

Then, she had a moment of abandon and stretched, extending the arm that had been on her waist and, in that opening, almost touching her cheek with the bicep. A soft shadow covered that part of Dina's face; and an even lighter one ran through her arm, but in both, the pale tonality of the flesh prevailed over the darkness with a silent challenge . . . without any flaps to confuse the arm with the side of the face.

I looked first at the sofa, and then at her vagina, which, together with her abdomen and thighs, absorbed the light of the small table lamp by her feet. I looked at her whole body again. "If I kiss her, I will end the singularity of this instant and the feeling it inspires in me."

I wasn't in front of a perfect body beyond the reach of time. She had a vaccine scar; her abdomen was too defined, because of her work; her underwear had left a rose mark just below the navel; and her feet were callused from so much standing in Corso di Porta Vigentina. But there was a totality to her beyond the details.

I had made a mistake concentrating only on a small fraction of skin on her arm that day when she was leaning on the bar, and I was making another mistake now by focusing on the calluses and the scars. Dina was beyond deconstruction; it was useless to try to deduce something from her lips or her abdominal muscles, because she was the very principle of unity. Every part of her body existed in consideration of the next. I remembered Nietzsche: "Your body and its great intelligence does not say 'I' but *performs* 'I.'" It was with all of her that I had to act, not with a phantasm, or fragments of her skin. I felt my body heat and the crotch of my pants grow tight, and I took a step toward her.

Dina knew that I was entranced. She shut her eyes and drew her lips closed. I took the stewardess's knife from my pocket, opened the blade without hesitating, and slashed her cheekbone. The bone flashed for a brief second before the blood appeared. I had enough time to cut again, before she opened her eyes in terror, not because of the attack, but because she couldn't understand what was happening. The scars would be visible, but not serious, I remember thinking.

—What did they pay you that day at the trattoria when I was made a fool with that whole *l'etto* story!

She buried her face in the plastic sofa, which didn't absorb the blood.

X

> Voice assumes mouth, eye, and finally face, a chain that is manifest in the etymology of the trope's name, "prosopon poien," to confer a mask or a face. Prosopopeia is the trope of autobiography, by which one's name is made as intelligible and memorable as a face. Our topic deals with the giving and taking away of faces, with face and deface, "figure," figuration and disfiguration.
>
> —Paul de Man

ELIGIA AND I TRAVELED home the next day. Behind, far below, Milan remained, mysterious and mine. Back home, the treatments went on a few more years: a scar was endlessly polished, and surgical touch-ups were made on Eligia's hands so she could open them comfortably.

Everyone praised the work of Professor Calcaterra, especially the local doctors, who wrote to Italy requesting photographs. One photo appeared in some journal article about reconstructive surgery, with a little black band across the eyes so no one could recognize her, or with zoomed-in sections of her face.

In the street, it was different. Children continued to stare at Eligia's skin—the uneven coloration, the unmolded forms—while the adults vomited their praise (clearly forced) about how beautiful she looked. Although the family offered her new places to live, she preferred to settle in Aron's apartment. For my part, I moved to a studio, three blocks away.

With the encouragement of all her friends and acquaintances, Eligia entered political life again, committed, as always, to the development of education. History played a curious surprise on her. In 1971, it was revealed, contrary to the reports of 1965, that the beautiful and intact cadaver of the General's wife had not been thrown into the ocean. This entire time the body had remained hidden in an anonymous tomb in Milan, not far from the clinic. Both women had been thousands of kilometers away from their country: one, perfect, eternal, buried, hidden under a false name; the other, destroyed, eager to get back to work, trying to regenerate her own body under everyone's astonished gaze.

Eligia's political party allied itself with the widowed General in the electoral battles that followed. She was appointed to campaign in the mountain provinces where her father had been governor, caudillo, and, first and foremost, enemy of the General.

Eligia confronted the dilemma between her father's memory and her certainty that nothing could be achieved without popular support. —I'm going to the mountains to campaign for the alliance—she told me. The party of Eligia's father was a declared opponent of her small party of technocrats. —They are going to attack me with everything they've got, but I don't see another way—she said. —Now is the moment for reconciliation and alliance.

It was 1973. The political map of our country was boiling after six years of de facto rule. They tried new combinations and pacts; new unexpected forces appeared. I, as always, didn't opine or act; every event disconcerted me more. It was better not to talk about my country, as Eligia had taught me in prison when I was ten. Better not to mention anything.

The political map created by my family was a moving labyrinth: Aron's parents had been conservatives; he had been a Stirnean anarchoindividualist; Eligia's father was a constitutionalist and fierce anti-Peronist; Eligia was a developmentalist, and therefore a member of the General's new alliance.

I accompanied her to the launch of the campaign in her province, in a small town. Even the smallest political party had scored a speaker, so the list was endless. When it was finally her turn, she delivered a short speech, citing detailed figures to demonstrate how education had regressed during the de facto governments. The audience paid no attention to her words, and when she pointed to the "increased grade repetition rate in primary school" as a damning fact against the last de facto government, a few smiles broke out across the crowd, mixed with sleepy nods and sighs.

The public was only interested in the courage of the speaker in the face of adversity, which was regarded as a much more important virtue than the analysis of educational statistics. But that personal and emotional touch was precisely what Eligia was never going to use. Had she made even an indirect reference to her suffering, she would have won the fervor of the people. But she never did.

They thanked her, recognizing her stoicism, but without the enthusiasm that courage demands. Their responses were steeped in rhetorical formulas. At least there was a roast afterward.

That night, the smell of crucified young goats invaded the classrooms of the school where the election campaign's launch was being celebrated. Eligia and I retired at two in the morning. As we crossed the courtyard, we passed near one of the fires. An old woman in her eighties spoke, surrounded by a crowd of peasants.

—I can testify about the Lady, the Lady the General sent to help and protect us. If you'd only seen her! She was blonde as the sun and very beautiful.

—This old woman worked for more than twenty years in the General's wife's sister's house—whispered one of the local politicians.

—The General loved her in life and also in death; and that's what the rest of us must do as well. The General had to leave when he was betrayed. His enemies took advantage and stole the Lady's body, which was already embalmed, as they say, and looked like the angel that she had always been. Only God knows what horrible things they did to her! But the Lady was stronger, and they weren't able to harm her, so they had to hide her. The body was hidden so well, there was no trace. She was missing for a long time, but then

she reappeared—on her own—and I was able to see her again, as blonde as ever; and though she also showed signs of her enemies' hate, she was white, angelic, and eternal. You wanted to touch her. "She's eternal," the doctor said who examined her. "Only fire or acid can destroy her." But I think not even fire or acid, for I am certain her enemies tried everything. I saw her myself when she reappeared: they had tried to cut her ear, they'd hit her face, they tried to destroy her nose and burned her feet, the poor angel! Her enemies didn't know—as we do—that beatings and fire purify. They didn't know that she had passed the test of fire before. My employer—her sister, who called me "comrade"—told me about a miracle from her youth. The two of them were playing one morning in the kitchen, very many years ago, when the Lady was only twelve ...

—Did you hear? She doesn't know it's improper to use "very" with "many"—I said to Eligia in a low voice. By this time, I was earning a living copyediting manuscripts. —Listen to her!

— *... the Lady was playing; she knocked a frying pan off the stove, and the oil burned the poor angel's entire body. There was a storm that morning. That's why they were playing in the kitchen. It was so painful, she couldn't even talk; there was just silence as the lightning flashed. Her sister thought nothing had happened. But when she touched her, she pulled back her hand fast as if she had touched an ember. The skin burned ... They took her to the village doctor, but science couldn't help, and her little body, only twelve years old, began to get darker, as if it were burning slowly from the inside. She became a walking scab, an image that scared all the other children. But one day the scab fell off, in one piece, and underneath there was a skin like no one had ever seen before; she was a Comrade kneaded in pain and burns. That's how it happened ... now, if we promise her the vote for these elections and we win,* *she will help and protect us forever; she will stay with her people for eternity, as it is said. And she will be miraculous, this Lady, because that is what we need.*

Eligia, who had come to the roast in good spirits and with a roll of written pages sticking out of her purse, took on an air of helpless passivity as the old woman talked. A few days later she resigned as spokesperson. During the rest of the electoral campaign, she supported the effort from a desk at the party's headquarters.

After the alliance won the elections, she rejected all offers for public office and decided to work on an international pedagogical research project. The objective was to conduct an analysis for UNESCO about the relationship between women's education and the labor supply. She selected a team of first-year university students, and they worked out of some offices provided by the Ministry of Education in the capital. When they finished, the woman in Czechoslovakia who had supervised the research congratulated the whole team and published the report as a model for similar studies around the world.

Fifteen months went by. One day, Eligia read in the newspaper that this woman was visiting our country. She called her hotel, and they made an appointment to see each other that same day. I tagged along, and as the three of us drove through the city, our guest was alarmed to see one of the protests; but we explained that this was typical of our local, political life. The woman calmed down and took several photos, savoring the sensation they would cause upon her return.

Later we sat down at a pastry shop. The two women talked

about shopping, but also about education. Finally, after breaking the ice over several cups of tea and pastry, the Czech woman came out with what was on her mind.

—There's something I don't understand. Three months after you finished the report, there was a high-level vacancy in UNESCO. I sent two letters to your ministry requesting your résumé, but my first letter went unanswered and, in response to the second one, they sent me the résumé of a twenty-three-year-old primary school teacher.

Eligia paused for a long time. A post at UNESCO was undoubtedly one of her dreams.

—I don't know what to tell you.

With the letter from our Ministry of Education, the résumé of the teacher applying for the post mentioned her knowledge of first aid and arts and crafts ... Eligia recognized her name as the employee in charge of distributing mail in the ministry's offices. The conclusion was obvious: the young woman had opened the letter addressed to Eligia after she no longer worked at the ministry, and decided to apply for the post without being asked.

After that episode, Eligia's professional activities slowed down and she focused on her medical treatment. One of the last details was the removal of the follicles from the interior of the eyelid, because some of the roots kept escaping electrical treatment and being reborn. Eligia was more concerned about these depilations than any of the more important surgeries. When the doctors were certain there wasn't a trace of hair left, they announced the end of the treatment. It had taken a year of emergency skin grafts in Argentina; twenty months in Italy with Professor Calcaterra; and more than twelve years upon her return, doing finishing touches on what the professor had started. Finally, all the doctors agreed: there was no point in seeking perfection, they had to put an end to a series of treatments that—considering all scientific possibilities—might as well be infinite.

For a few years, Eligia devoted her time to administering a piece of land and visiting friends in the most remote regions of the pampas. Almost all of them were teachers, but if Eligia accompanied them to their schools, the students couldn't help but stare in stunned silence.

One afternoon in October of 1978, Eligia showed me an album with photos from her days as a functionary, before Aron had vitriolated her. A photographer had captured an image of her raising a flag or delivering one of her speeches. She looked happy in the photos. Anxiously, she asked me:

—What do I do with all this?

I didn't know what to say. We were sitting in the same library where Aron had thrown the acid and where I am writing this ... The old Louis XVI armchairs had been replaced, but the black lacquer and cherry of the desk and chest on the small table remained—as did the acid stains on the floorboards beneath the new cheap carpet.

—And this?

She opened the chest, where she had stored mementos of her own, including a letter one of our relatives sent to Italy. Also inside—although there was plenty of space on the shelves, because I had sold all of Aron's French pornography as soon as we returned from Milan, and she hadn't filled the gaps with her bulky volumes on history and pedagogy—were some of the books and magazines I'd read to Eligia twelve years ago, including the issue with the description of the battle. There was also a photo of Santa Maria delle Grazie from the perspective of our window in Milan, napkins with the clinic's letterhead, recipes from Professor Calcaterra, and a prayer card with the image of the Madonna (the golden Virgin, standing high atop the Duomo in Milan) given to her by the priest.

I never imagined she could have felt any fondness for that time. In the same chest, Aron had kept the compositions of his children under his and Eligia's old papers. Close to the top was an essay that I had presented at a literary conference about the impossibility of lyric poetry in our times. It had been a vain attempt to get an assistant faculty position, despite not having a university degree. My monographs were ridiculed by young professors, who assured me my point of view was past its time.

—So what do I do with this? —she insisted, looking at the open chest. Again, I didn't know what to say.

The next day Eligia jumped from a window in the apartment that had also been Aron's, though they had never lived there together. The trajectory of her fall was from east to west, facing the Dome where the sun sets.

XI

ONE MONTH LATER, IN November of 1978, I bumped into an academic I had met at a publishing house, who'd mentioned that he was interested in Aron and his novels. We went to a bar and sat down to discuss them.

The man was young, barely forty, and possessed the kind of self-assurance that I so envied in my compatriots, but could never imitate.

—You don't remember me? —he asked. —I used to work at May Publishing House, when you copyedited those cookbook pamphlets. You were famous because you raced through the stuff and never missed a thing.

—In all modesty, I'm a pro.

—Well, fame is one thing, the truth is another. In that collection of recipes you forgot to make sure the actual recipes preceded the lists of ingredients. When you finished the job and the pamphlets were published, random grandmothers started calling us for clarification: "How do I prepare the three hundred grams of tuna?" "What do I do with the four thinly sliced radishes?" There were no spelling errors, but the culinary syntax had every hole ...

—I needed the work.

—Oh, you don't need to tell me. But in the recipes, you mixed up all the beans: garbanzo, fava, kidney, black, pinto ... Is it all the same to you?

—They're more or less the same, no? I still can't tell them apart ... I do know all the names, but I'd forget which was black-eyed, lima, navy, soy, white, green, carob, and about fifty others; in my dictionary, they're all the same: "the edible seed of a leguminous plant, typically kidney-shaped, growing in long pods." So how do you expect me to tell them apart?

The conversation was making me uncomfortable, so I changed the subject.

—So you're telling me you're interested in those operatic pornographic novels? What makes you think anyone would publish this kind of thing now?

The General had died, and the military was in power again.

—Mario, they were pornographic forty years ago, but things have changed. The reception now would be entirely different. As for the present—and he lowered his voice—all of this will also change. You see, I am not really interested in pure literary technique; what I'm really after is the sociosemiotic meanings of these texts. The narrator in Aron Gageac's novels is just an object, the signified subject of the text, which, with the word's semantic candor, carries a series of literary signs and transposes them almost without transcodification, excepting its tendency toward sublimation. In Gageac's case, the process of sublimation produces ideals in the first books ... and resentments in the latter, especially the one he completed the year of his death.

—I haven't read it. How is it?

—It is ... uh, bad.

He continued his analysis, as if all the technical jargon could protect him from any discomfort: —If we look at Gageac's early works (which coincide with the author's first steps into political action), we can apply some of the current concepts in the literary critiques of novelists from the thirties. According to this analysis, the characters embody a deep disappointment that mirrors the world of that decade, a world that hadn't become the utopia so many of these authors expected. You know, the crisis of the 1930s and all that ... The degradation of literary characters through this decade reflects the degradation of the authors themselves. Both the characters and authors abandoned the prestigious status of heroes that had been conferred on them just fifteen or twenty years before. Instead, they turn to a perverse solitude, detached from their former values, which are now ruins. In this debris, they built a different ego, one feeding on completely personal syntactical combinations. In Gageac's case, the collapse of his former self took place during a period when the privileged subjects of enunciation were returning with all their power and riches. But Gageac, either by his own choice or the self-critical decision typical of members of his class ... "

—What? —I asked confused.

— ... I mean that either he sent his friends to shit—or the other way around ... Gageac's self-exclusion from his social class is unique in this country of fanatics and social climbers, so his case is interesting from a sociological perspective.

He hesitated, looked me in the eyes, and continued.

—On the diachronic plane, considering his evolution, the form is more psychiatric than sociological. The fact that his last book was illustrated by a painter who later tried to assassinate the Pope demonstrates precisely the power of paranoia—subconscious, iconoclastic—in Gageac's resentments, which were really a warning about the direction the country was taking. In him, these resentments are manifested against his own social class, during his political activity in the 1930s; but then, in the 1960s, they reemerge without any ideological garb, as the author was transformed into *an emitter* of resentment and provocation against every ideal. It is the failure of the great discourses and universal reason that was promised by the Enlightenment ...

—Sorry ... What is an "emitter?"

—"Emitter" has a more expansive sense than "enunciator."

—Meaning? ...

—Well, if you agree with J. L. Austin, it's something close to "locutor," which opposes "alocutory" and "delocutory."

—I don't know Austin.

—Then we must start with the *actantial* categories. In this context we could talk about a "sender," who sends letters ...

—Is that good or bad?

—Good? Bad? Don't tell me you still don't have a grasp of these oppositions! You speak as if you believed in the subject of knowledge and ethics! Are you an idealist?

—No! I know even less about Kant ...

—Or worse, you're not a humanist, are you? He looked at me with a hint of pity.

—No ... How could I be! I couldn't even finish my studies in the humanities! If only I had listened to my old lady. I could go on and on about all the jobs I've lost just because I don't know Latin. I would be rich by now, and thousands of kilometers away from the famous Aron Gageac and all his "emissions" …

—Listen, what I need is some information. Do you know if there were any reviews of his books in the newspapers?

—None. Not even to destroy him. They crossed him out from literary circles as a contrarian and class traitor. Don't forget that the son of our national poet was the police chief in those days. When he assumed the position, Aron was in prison because he had tried to organize a coup. Let's just say the chief took care of him personally. What a duo! No?

—Are any of Gageac's friends still alive?

—None. His friendships only lasted weeks, a few months at most. He would bitch everyone out. In the end, he was almost completely alone.

—Did you keep the books from his library?

—None of them. I sold the ones that were worth anything. Don't look at me like that, you know that I went through hard times, entire weeks on just gin and rice. Sometimes I couldn't even afford hot dogs. When you're stuck with an old man who thinks he's the Marquis de Sade and spends all his money building monuments to his passions, you end up eating rice and hot dogs … What was I supposed to do? I live in a studio. It was a massive book collection, and I couldn't even move his crazy furniture.

—What about his letters? Journals? Were there unfinished manuscripts?

—None. He burned most of his stuff before he committed suicide … On that note, could you lend me your copy of his last book?

—Look, it's no good. It will fall apart in your hands.

—I just want to take a look. I'm curious.

—Actually, I lent my copy to someone.

THE MADWOMAN FROM THE ATTIC DOESN'T GIVE UP

THE DIFFICULTIES OF LYRIC POETRY AND THE DEMANDS OF THE MARKETPLACE

The "lyrical attitude," which is one possibility of man's existence—Goethe called man in this condition the "natural species"—has been hit hard by the recent metastasis of the markets…

Lyrical poetry (one can still refer to Wolgang Kayser) was born in the fusion of subject and object. This possibility is presented to us as one of the existential paths unifying being, along with religiosity, idiocy, or artificially altered states of consciousness. The widening of some of these paths—such as artificially altered states or idiocy—reveals the disappearance of others, such as mysticism or lyrical poetry.

Like everything that is essentially human, lyrical work is a solitary endeavor and thus unappreciated as long as the culture industry isn't able to possess or distort it. This capitalist assault on the heart of man has been resisted by artists in strategic retirement; despite the fact that poetry does not sell, artists create works that leave nothing tangible behind (happenings, performances). Today's philosophies associate the lyrical with the negation of plurality, an irrational elitism. The vaccine is Goethe.

The German thinker was opposed to art as the product of unleashed will, even before Schlegel theorized the absolute "I" of Romantic irrationality. Goethean lyrical poetry is born from a unique form of knowledge. In order to determine the nature of this knowl-

edge, it is helpful to remember Karl Löwith, who emphasizes two aspects of Goethean thought: first, the creative and autonomous character of lyrical feeling, always referred to as that contributing to a collective work (the "barbarian" cathedral of Strasbourg or the popular song), not resulting from pantheistic and absolute I; second: the lyrical recognizes itself in a Nature (in Goethe's case, the Mediterranean of Antiquity) that represents, in his vision, the doing and suffering of man in a perceptible unity: "in unison, man captures the world from himself and himself from the world."

The lyrical dispenses with all social relations; however, it is self-sufficient, emitted and received in solitude in a sacred intimacy. Its voice is a silence full of negative meanings: it does not pretend for love to be resolved in sex; it does not pretend for death to hide in eternal consumption; it does not pretend for melancholy to be distracted by tourism. The lyrical only applies to its immediate surroundings, because the lyrical attitude is born without dialogue; it is grounded in the boundary between silence and the scream ...

The lyrical at its core remains oblivious to time and contradiction. From it comes eccentricity, the destruction of logic, grammar, rationality, because in its capacity to bring about actualization, it never yields to systematization ...

Although today's university students don't pay attention to the lyrical phenomenon, the powerful on earth recognize it immediately for its capacity to disrupt the entire system, credits and TV included. This characteristic of the genre we are analyzing is dominant, precisely because it has no intention to reinvent or transgress anything, much less to dominate or sell itself. Lyrical poetry never trusted History, Progress, Revolution, the Market, or Culture. It realizes the ideal of meeting with Nature and our fellow beings, without destroying itself or surmounting them. None of this applies to those words with capital letters. Only the mystical offers a similar attitude.

The lyrical is enunciated as a high offer left to chance, with no expectations of being received. It evades mass communication and, frequently, the personal. It offers itself without conditions, indicated by the predisposition of the subject and not the market, and instead of submitting to demand, it presents itself before freedom.

XII

January ?, 1979

I RETURN TO THE apartment where Aron and Eligia lived, opening the windows to let some fresh air into the place. Torrents of heat move through the rooms. I've come to take the objects that belonged to Eligia, before the place is put up for sale.

Going through the kitchen cabinets and the dining room, I occupy myself with unimportant things. The whole place smells like still air and mold, without trace of food or spices. I find a few bottles of cheap liquor that Eligia used for desserts, and one, almost finished, of whiskey, the same peaty Scotch that Aron used to drink. It would be more trouble to take all these bottles with me, so I decide to drink them.

When the sun begins to set, its light filters through the dry branches of shrubs that no one has watered on the balcony since October; I decide to go into the library to pack the few remaining books. Finally, I open the chest. Under my essay—at an uncertain stratigraphic level—I find Aron's last novel. It's hard to tell who put it there.

I read it while working on a translucent, pomegranate-colored liquor, before moving on to a dark, thick one. The book is a product of absolute resentment. What in the 1930s had been praised as Aron's "willingness to go all in" ends up becoming, at the beginning of the sixties, a shouting match with himself: he hates women, athletes, the Pope, Jews, his readers, the Yankees, revolutionaries, his friends, businessmen, journalists, pretentious people, servile people, gypsies, intellectuals...

The book reads: "Why not deny one's son begotten more out of curiosity than desire? What obligation is there to love one's newborn? Let him be burdened with his own shame, rather than I with his forgiveness."

I try to imagine what place I could possibly have in that text, and I find none. Everything that binds me to those printed words I reject. Indignation makes me wince. I reread some of the passages: Aron went much further than being a drunk, he built a space where it is impossible to recognize any limits.

I've opened a desert with no boundaries, a breed of evil no longer needing to express itself through aggression, because it has locked itself in an orb where nothing that could be called human exists: a narcissistic world that self-generates, and lacerates all relations, all perspective, any reunification. He chose to stare into the void—the eye of futility—to create where no defect can be admitted, because to recognize a defect is to admit there is such a thing as perfection. The eye of futility... To reach the desert voluntarily, Aron retraced his love for Eligia, as well as his salvageable, political trajectory from the thirties.

There is a difference between his relationship to these two crucial things—women and politics. His aggression toward the feminine rested on selfish motives. Like all the men of his day, he acted as if he were superior to all others when it came to women, and from a young age, he resented them when he couldn't be their one and only lover.

But on the political plane, he seemed to be on the right track: he was altruistic. Why did he attack everything he fought for?

Already lacking lucidity, I try to sketch an explanation. His first outbursts, I suppose, originated from an authentic though contradictory feeling against his social class. Not finding a worthy opponent in politics—the way he found one in his beloved—he launched an attack against *all* ideals, with more ingenuity than planning. He was arrested and beaten. He encountered hate, which he preferred to any ideal; they would never separate. To make matters worse, during the toughest years of the 1930s, he was one of the few who actually fought back. And when those infamous times passed, Aron's own partisans avoided him because of his violent temperament. They thus refused to recognize any of his victories. Even old Presotto, Eligia's father, a governor, had him arrested on conspiracy charges; he ordered his men to break into his property and the little school he had for his staff, where Eligia taught her first few classes. There they found two hundred rifles hidden in an enormous tomb, "two hundred feet deep," where he'd kept the burnt corpse of his first wife—who was killed during an air raid. As soon as he got out of jail, Aron married Presotto's daughter—she was only sixteen—and thus he combined his political resentment with his sexual megalomania. When Aron decided to leave forever—twenty-eight years later—he wrote the book that I am now holding...

This explanation does not satisfy me, but any other would seem equally insufficient. Between the man who built schools for children and monuments to those he loved and the one who threw acid at his beloved, there is a transformation that I cannot understand. My inability to comprehend him is what binds us.

Over and over again, I think about the connection between Aron's aberrant ideological fall, his separation from Eligia, and the acid he threw on her. "How could anyone hurt a defenseless woman?" I ask myself stupefied.

Aron wrote this book while I was living with him. I try to remember those times. We barely talked, but we drank a lot. I always hated his writings, and strove to distinguish myself from him, but I willingly shared the insane atmosphere of his apartment, and perhaps contributed to it. *Now* my options are: a parricide of his memory, to be resentful by inheritance, but without wealth; or to be a vulgar imitator with the bottle and the bullet. I mustn't remain solely a negative consequence of Aron. I must turn this story around.

How could Aron have hurt a woman who had loved him so much, as I had done twice myself, in Milan, with Eligia and Dina? Aron's storm brews inside me. All these reflections regarding Aron also apply to me. It seems this is the only door he left half-open. I understand this opening into the abyss will remain with me for the rest of my life, yet I don't know what I will do. Above all, I don't know what it will do to me.

I want to move; it's past midnight. I throw the face creams and special makeup in a garbage bag. In the same cabinet, I find a few bottles of Aron's cologne. After fourteen years, the smell is even more potent. All his stuff is there. For twelve years, Eligia lived in that apartment; she didn't move or get rid of a single thing. Even his old razor still has hair from its last use.

I go into the bedroom. The drawers are lined with Eligia's austere blouses, and, underneath, Aron's yellowed dress shirts, with the hard necks and cuffs that were already anachronistic in the sixties. In the armoire, I find her *tailleurs* next to his double-breasted gangster suits. The objects stayed together for those last twelve years.

A strong doubt suddenly assails me. Did she read his last book? I compare the dates. "Impossible!" I say to myself, relieved; it was printed a few days before the attack and never distributed—as will probably be the fate of this text. But the volume did remain in the chest for the twelve years Eligia lived in the apartment. Did she read it, abhorring the book, while loving the man? What confusing emotions must she have felt? Or was she wise enough to not even open the thing? Is there candor once you decide to coexist with evil? What are these territories that no one ever talks about? "If one loves another who doesn't deserve it, sooner or later, the greatness of that love will transform the other into someone worthy of that love." Forget these damn sermons! What happens if "sooner or later" is beyond life and understanding? I am at the exact point where God is no longer something in a sermon, but a necessity. I ask for mercy in His intelligent wrath, that it may take my random, grotesque story somewhere good at last.

I go back to the library and out onto the balcony covered with dry leaves. I glance at the dome in the shadows and the trees in the middle of the block. Thirty meters below is the garden where Eligia fell and Professor Calcaterra's skills ended. Some reflections allow me to see the "ladies of the night" and the blossoming geraniums: only fragments. A chain is pulling me toward the void. Neither Aron nor Eligia seemed free after their suicides. I reject this, and a rich sense of possibility comes over me. I remember walking down a hill in the dark, thousands of kilometers from this library.

I might have started calling Eligia "mother," or something like "mom" really, that is how it would all start. No matter how many grafts and flaps Eligia had to suffer in Milan, she always found the strength to curl her finger around mine, to smile at me—timidly, forced—without lips, and that was her only way of smiling. It was in *her* that Aron conceived me, whether I like it or not. John's interpretation, as relayed by the priest in Milan, is wrong; no flesh can be indifferent. The flesh carries pleasure or suffering. In both cases, it implicates another person—a lover or torturer—and any destiny they share. Ultimately, evil has a will, but so does our time, however insufficient that may be.

I go back into the library and stare at the empty shelves. At thirty-six, I'm convinced that I have wasted everything. If the time of metaphors ended for me twelve years ago, now the time for excuses is over. In the last few months I haven't encountered anything vital, save this decision to step back from the balcony into the bare library. The only thing to come to me at the crossroads since Eligia's suicide is a few books, some for consolation, others that overwhelm me. My health won't hold up with this hope I have summoned; I have removed myself too much from life. I am vomiting every day. Sooner or later all that will remain of my life is just a text. I don't have much left to do. I write these lines. This fragile impulse to create is the only thing that could still be called "life," or "action," or "possibility."

I seek refuge in the memory of Dina. In her own way, she took care of others—the lovers and torturers—or, as it often happened, a confused mix of both. She bowed to the needs of those who desired her; she caressed them the way they wanted; she even stole from them, when that was the behavior they expected. With me, she appeared and disappeared with angelic exactitude, always taking my hand, guiding and leaving me somewhere decisive, so I could—if I wanted—stand up and embrace her. When she realized I wasn't capable of that, she lost her angelic, ghostly quality and loved me, but I destroyed her ... I feel the weight of her image returning after being dormant for so long. My blood boils to becoming indignant. What I am talking about is reconciliation.

THE END

AFTERWORD

ON SUNDAY AUGUST 16, 1964, Raúl Barón Biza met with his wife Clotilde Sabattini and their respective lawyers in his apartment on 1256 Esmeralda Street in Buenos Aires. The purpose of the meeting was to finalize the details of a divorce that had been thirty years in the works since their wedding in Uruguay. Jorge Barón Biza—one of three children from the marriage who, during the intermittent separations that fanned Clotilde's feminism, also went by Jorge Barón Sabattini—described his parents' bond as an amalgamation of love and hate, "a passionate, infinite divorce." In a short letter to the editor of the newspaper *Clarín* published in 1986, and in his posthumous book *Everything Is Allowed Inside*, Jorge writes the following in response to a journalistic investigation of his family by Enrique Sdrech: "Separation is an unthinkable fact when there is only love and it is the easiest recourse when there is just hate. But it is a messy heartbreak when love and hate are one and the same confused element fueling passion in our hearts." That pain that the son invokes in the royal pronoun, to warn of and to comprehend the criminal twists of his family history, had its unexpected culmination that afternoon in the year 1964 in Emerald Street, when Raúl, after pouring whiskey for his guests, flung the contents of a glass at Clotilde's face. It was acid: corrosive, muriatic, hydrochloric, sulfuric, vitriol... there are many variations in the many alternate accounts of that afternoon, all, with an equal result. Clotilde's face was finished; and the disintegration, so immediate at first, continued to bore through her identity hour after hour. That same day, shortly after the lawyers rushed the woman to the hospital, Raúl changed into his silk robe, laid down in bed, and shot himself.

Without this grand anecdote that brought him fame and infamy, and that also sent him into oblivion, the life of Raúl Barón Biza is reduced to a list of ways adversaries and admirers used to describe him: rich boy, world traveler, party-loving and depressive Don Juan, a monumental widower, landlord, squanderer, excommunicated and radical insurgent, political prisoner, hunger striker, expat, duelist, entrepreneur, pornographer, blasphemer, frequent defendant, on-and-off ambassador, art dealer, a *robe de chambre* suicide. In his son's account, however, his peripatetic, miserable life is abstracted, under the name Aron Gageac, into a single compound of violence, ideals, and courage, a father figure to be rejected. In *The Desert and Its Seed*, Jorge includes three fragments from Raúl's novels: *Why I Became a Revolutionary* (1934), *Final Period* (1941), and *Everything Was Dirty* (1963). Even though he saw an apocalyptic originality in them, for the most part he considered them narcissistic, resentful, and clichéd. Perhaps he included them as a counterpoint, to illustrate his father's lumpen literature.

Clotilde Sabattini, who also moves—albeit along different

paths—on a trajectory toward abstraction, becomes, in her son's novel, Eligia, and what remains of a face when there is no more face. Her life as an intellectual, the daughter of the radical leader and eventual governor of Cordoba, Amadeo Sabattini, the young militant woman, the school teacher, outstanding student in foreign universities, the president of the first congress of radical women, the political prisoner and exile under Peronism, the high-ranking education officer in Frondizi's government, author of the first Teachers' Statute, the woman whose fatigue drew her to suicide, are all summed up, in this novel, by her nose—the nose that is the product of cosmetic surgery and stands as a point of resistance to the destruction of her face. There is her "nostalgia of teaching," and also as a counterpoint, the ravages of her living body, traced against the embalmed corpse of Eva Perón, both spoils of a historical feud.

The son, Jorge—Jorge Barón Sabattini, Jorge Barón Biza—born into a fortune but without one, proofreader, ghost writer, journalist, teacher, art critic, translator of Proust, extraordinary author of a single novel, precocious alcoholic, suicide-by-a-fall, is the young Mario Gageac (Gageac from the Aquitaine of France, where the Barón lineage came from; they boasted—per Christian Ferrer's account in *Barón Biza, The Immoralist*—about having a fifteenth-century castle).

The family's noble lineage and legend were repeatedly recounted by journalists of the time and reiterated by subsequent researchers. The autobiographical accuracy of *The Desert and Its Seed* is best described by the author's response to Ferrer: "The novel is obviously autobiographical but it is not confessional." So, what exactly is this difference that Barón points out to his pen pal, a scholar of the ideological byways of his father?

First, there is the trimming of an important sequence of the family story: *The Desert and Its Seed* begins where the melodrama concludes, as indicated in the novel's opening line, "Moments after the attack ..." The author focuses not on the lives of his parents spilling into torrents and leading to that moment, but on a posthumous description of that passionate plunder. The swift discarding of small vicissitudes in favor of describing the pure vestiges is at times very prudent and measured, but prudence and moderation have little to do with the narrative art the author puts to the test here. Because it is not intrigue that matters, nor its absurd development, or resolution; in Barón Biza, in the calibrated time span of his narrative, nothing *else* happens. His wager, artistic and lived, resides in *reconstructing* (the author's verb par excellence) the avatars of his history, so that the son is imposed, from the beginning, to write a novel without material; one, that painfully begins where it has already ended.

Second—and this order, of course, is arbitrary: with this account comes the instantaneous combustion of its components—we must consider the choice of the formerly drifting narration in the first person, with its remarkably active viewpoint. Mario Gageac does not for a moment condescend to redemptive tribulations, which are so typical of confessional moralism. The young narrator of *The Desert and Its Seed*, who accompanies Eligia to Milan and assists her through her series of facial surgeries, maintains a stubborn distance, a scrupulous perspective, on the burning drama of his autobiographical matter. There is no fiction, no life, without that vantage point; the narrative act always depends on the solidity of this point of view, one that can structure a group of events into a plot.

What is exceptional and artistically grand about Barón Biza is this very formal perspective that precipitates form, content, and matter in the very process of reconstruction. Only in this way can the novel's autobiographical character come about: not in the many coincidences (certain, desperate) between the author's fictional and truthful accounts, but in the tenor of his narrative voice, his foci, the panoramas, his brief moments of wisdom, and, above all, the potent sobriety of his distance and questioning. Barón Biza defines this attitude (with his usual genius for the paradoxical) as "the constructive collapse of the enigma": *what happened? why did it happen?* and, most importantly, *how could it have happened?* are questions that ultimately don't lead to a revelation. But Barón Biza, who is a master of the enigma without suspense, uses these questions as the narrative scaffolding of the novel.

Mario Gageac configures a surface wherein his story can advance, tracing a trajectory that allows him to confront, as a privileged observer, the enormity of a detonation, an expanse without hermeneutic depth; his narrative impulse for realism is so powerful, it ultimately corrupts any verisimilitude: "her features clearly indicated that something impossible had occurred to her: no matter how intense her suffering, her reality was no longer convincing." Eligia's face is no longer the Romantic or realistic reflection of the soul, that rich field of diegetic representation. This is not due to her calm fortitude, a psychic trick, or French objectivism, but because her features disintegrated in the act, and her gestures have become "inexpressive like the desert." The face of the mother thus entirely loses its faculty to manifest her reversal of fortune: no parable, just "pure facticity." "I understood," writes Barón with prodigious clarity, "that the mirage of metaphor was over." With this unstable form of substance, there is no redemptive arbitration of meaning. No transcendence, no lesson, no confessional pretext, no lifeline, no "smiling humanism," as Aron would have called it. Barón Biza's remark abstracts the tragedy by presenting its material effects, and *only* its material effects — "the distance," writes Paul de Man, quoted by Barón Biza in one of the epigraphs, "which protects the autobiographical author from his own experience."

In a series of lectures delivered in Zurich in 1997, and published under the title *On the Natural History of Destruction*, W. G. Sebald proposed a single way, both artistic and testimonial, to communicate a catastrophe: to narrate it in its "pure facticity." And although here Sebald is thinking of entire German populations being annihilated by aerial wars, the relative calamity of Eligia's face in *The Desert and Its Seed* can be thought of in similar terms: a territory lethally attacked. Against allegory, redemption, and all enigmatic language (in Barón Biza, the "constructive collapse of the enigma" always dominates), what resists the impulse toward description—not because of its impenetrability but because of its absolute clarity—must be narrated without the help of metaphor. Here, on the disastrous surface, the value of Sebald's "pure facticity" lies in returning to the concrete power of instantaneous destruction without the detriment of testimonies full of remains, morals, or imprecations. Jorge Barón Biza, a survivor, knows this point of view very well, and, in his narrative, he transforms it into an attitude; that is, he imbues his perspective with a visual ethos that doesn't circumvent formal details (lines, textures, volume, color, folds, crevices), at the same time not emptying them them of expression and, above all, of a final and restorative meaning.

Eligia's ravaged face lacks a spiritual underside. True fortitude, does not treasure the life inside, but only the Baroque caverns of "folds," "abysses," "crevices," "contours and colors," "flaps," "tiny streams of blood," "cavities," "darkening scabs," and, in the background, emerging by the action of the acid and surgeries, the inconvenient skull: a complete geology of the cataclysm. But Mario Gageac is also devoid of an emotional undercurrent; there is nothing to examine in the depths of his character, no inner monologue, no deep psychology. "I practiced apathy from early on," he says. Eligia's silence is almost total (except for the occasional moan or short sentence). She barely speaks, and, if there are voices in her head, the novel makes a conscious decision not to register them. Mario, in his narrative eloquence moves in the same direction, in latitudes that, though serpentine and irregular, don't delve into hidden motives, because, as Mario and Eligia would probably assert in their own way, the skin is the deepest. Hence the act of description—at once removed yet detailed, even with some naturalistic and aestheticizing features—is the most powerfully executed element in *The Desert and Its Seed*: Eligia's face is a paradigm, but, so are the hospital room, the streets, an alcove, a garden, the fog, and the facade of the University in Milan; Arcimboldi's canvas; the architecture of the churches, the cemeteries, the hills, the Italian countryside; the naked body of Dina (the prostitute Mario accompanies in their sordid adventures). "I looked around," writes Barón Biza. "The aesthetic appreciation that Mr. Bormann instilled in me and I accepted with such pride is now receding into incomprehensible spaces."

The *language* of this novel unfolds in this materialist sense, that rare unrepresentational pidgin, ever so delicate, crafted for a single speaker, in which Barón Biza's characters speak and deliberate. "A made-up language" — says Barón — that allows him to point out, with sheer syntax and lexical touches, the foreignness of Italians or Australians and a certain Argentine "Pancriollismo" (regionalism), provincial and Peronist. The idiolects work together: the lesser ones intermittently taking over the dominant, so that the Spanish tongue is rarefied in this grafting of languages and, as Eligia's face transforms, it unfolds in an "malicious cadence." "It is thus generated," writes Barón in a 1999 article, "*La Libertad del Cocoliche*" ("The Freedom of Pidgin Languages"), "a principle that doesn't come from a norm, but from a struggle between expression, ignorance and experience." The result is a language in motion, with great locution and vigor, that greatly exceeds the purpose of signaling foreignness, provincialism or social class, establishing a style in this tension between voice and experience. As in the description of the mother's face, here the process of reconstruction also works, leaning toward linguistic innovation with an autonomy and freedom that is even more astonishing because it originates from the most coercive mandate: the inheritance of both a mother tongue and this tragedy.

In the tradition of the great Argentine autobiographers, from Sarmiento to Victoria Ocampo, Barón Biza links his family history to that of the country. From his father's years as a revolutionary—the 1930s, after the coup, when he had his moment as an Yrigoyenist radical leader—Jorge transcribes in *The Desert and Its Seed* the 1933 speech "The Time to Fight Has Come" (which is included in the book *Why I Became a Revolutionary*, where Raúl calls for resistance against the fascist right). In the novel, of course, it is written by Arón Gageac. But beyond this quoted passage and a small graft of the father's books into the son's, the narrative also establishes a parallel between the bodies of Eligia and "the General's wife," a historical counterpoint between Clotilde Sabattini and Eva Perón. On one hand, there are the workings of the acid and the medical proceedings on Eligia's face; on the other, Eva's captive corpse, molded into the fragile, intact beauty of an incorruptible doll; and, in a "curious trick" of history, the two are both in the city of Milan: one in a clinic, the other in an "anonymous tomb."

"Eva Perón and Clotilde Sabattini were the same age," writes Christian Ferrer, "they were born within six months of each other and appear in the same moment in history, in opposite parties, both young women with plenty of courage." But the courage of these two women is also opposite. In *The Desert and Its Seed*, Eligia, with "her naïve and technocratic soul," challenges, in her public life, the "the energetic style of the General's wife." The two thus embody the spirit of their respective organizations, one, the radical, "studious and reasonable," and the other "fiery," the Peronist.

There is something about the respective victory and political defeat of this female duo that is perhaps the only allegory Barón Biza allows himself. Although Mario Gageac in presenting these two opposite women, elevates Eligia (a character without a mythology), he still punctures this comparison, measuring Eva's popularity and transcendence in magnitudes of two hundred thousand clamoring bodies, next to Eligia's forty. That popularity has, toward the end of Mario's account, its own Peronist voice; it is also conveyed in inimitable pidgin, an imaginary mixture of provincial dialects, which bears witness, in action and through the years, to the victory of one party, one style, one woman over the other: "'She's eternal,' said the doctor who examined Eva, 'Only fire or acid can destroy her ... but I think not even fire or acid.'"

Jorge Barón Biza was born in Buenos Aires on May 22, 1942, and committed suicide in the city of Córdoba on September 9, 2001. In 1995, he finished writing *The Desert and Its Seed.* Two years later he submitted it for the Premio Planeta de Novela, a Spanish literary prize, under the title *The Laws of a Silence.* It was not even selected. In 1998 he used his own money to print the first edition and made up his own autobiography on the book jacket:

> A great current of condolences followed the first suicide in my family. When the second happened, the current became a swaying ocean with no horizons. After the third, people run to close the window every time I go into a room that's more than three stories high. My solitude got caught in sequences like this.
>
> Otherwise, I was born in 1942, I came of age in schools, bars, editorial departments, madhouses, and museums in Buenos Aires, Fribourg in Sarine, Rosario, Villa María, La Falda, Montevideo, Milan, and New York. I read Mann, I translated Proust. For thirty years, I worked as a proofreader, ghostwriter, journalist (everything from psychiatric sanatorium publications to high society magazines), and an art critic.

NORA AVARO

BUENOS AIRES, 2013